ALLEN COU...

P9-ECT-188

3 1833 04442 9576

"It's a rational decision. Help me pull it off."

Winnie met Rand's gaze squarely.

He held her gaze another long second, then he gave his head a short, quick nod. "One emergency landing strip coming up." He turned to his window, beginning his search for an open stretch of land.

A small thread of relief slid through her. Getting them down in one piece was going to be hard enough without her passenger fighting her on every decision. And it felt good to have him on her side.

There was something about the man—an air of danger, of confidence—that made her think he'd been in tight situations before. And if he was confident she could get them down, maybe they *were* going to squeak out of this ugly situation… and get on with their lives!

ROMANCE

Dear Reader,

Welcome to more juicy reads from Silhouette Special Edition. I'd like to highlight Silhouette veteran and RITA® Award finalist Teresa Hill, who has written over ten Silhouette books under the pseudonym Sally Tyler Hayes. Her second story for us, *Heard It Through the Grapevine,* has all the ingredients for a fast-paced read—marriage of convenience, a pregnant preacher's daughter and a handsome hero to save the day. Teresa Hill writes, "I love this heroine because she takes a tremendous leap of faith. She hopes that her love will break down the hero's walls, and she never holds back." Don't miss this touching story!

USA TODAY bestselling and award-winning author Susan Mallery returns to her popular miniseries HOMETOWN HEARTBREAKERS with *One in a Million.* Here, a sassy single mom falls for a drop-dead-gorgeous FBI agent, but sets a few ground rules—a little romance, no strings attached. Of course, we know rules are meant to be broken! Victoria Pade delights us with *The Baby Surprise,* the last in her BABY TIMES THREE miniseries, in which a confirmed bachelor discovers he may be a father. With encouragement from a beautiful heroine, he feels ready to be a parent...and a husband.

The next book in Laurie Paige's SEVEN DEVILS miniseries, *The One and Only* features a desirable medical assistant with a secret past who snags the attention of a very charming doctor. Judith Lyons brings us *Alaskan Nights,* which involves two opposites who find each other irritating, yet totally irresistible! Can these two survive a little engine trouble in the wilderness? In *A Mother's Secret,* Pat Warren tells of a mother in search of her secret child and the discovery of the man of her dreams.

This month is all about love against the odds and finding that special someone when you least expect it. As you lounge in your favorite chair, lose yourself in one of these gems!

Sincerely,

Karen Taylor Richman
Senior Editor

Please address questions and book requests to:
Silhouette Reader Service
U.S.: 3010 Walden Ave., P.O. Box 1325, Buffalo, NY 14269
Canadian: P.O. Box 609, Fort Erie, Ont. L2A 5X3

Alaskan Nights

Judith Lyons

SPECIAL EDITION™

Published by Silhouette Books

America's Publisher of Contemporary Romance

If you purchased this book without a cover you should be aware that this book is stolen property. It was reported as "unsold and destroyed" to the publisher, and neither the author nor the publisher has received any payment for this "stripped book."

Many thanks to all the people who helped with the research on this book. My darling brother, Dave Morgan, fly fisherman extraordinaire. My Alaskan connection, Kay and Rich Aber, pilots and friends. And last, but certainly not least, many, many thanks to my wonderful husband, who not only kept my heroine flying the proper airplane for the job, but is an endless source of support when deadlines loom both large and small. Thanks, sweetie.

 SILHOUETTE BOOKS

ISBN 0-373-24547-5

ALASKAN NIGHTS

Copyright © 2003 by Julie M. Higgs

All rights reserved. Except for use in any review, the reproduction or utilization of this work in whole or in part in any form by any electronic, mechanical or other means, now known or hereafter invented, including xerography, photocopying and recording, or in any information storage or retrieval system, is forbidden without the written permission of the editorial office, Silhouette Books, 233 Broadway, New York, NY 10279 U.S.A.

All characters in this book have no existence outside the imagination of the author and have no relation whatsoever to anyone bearing the same name or names. They are not even distantly inspired by any individual known or unknown to the author, and all incidents are pure invention.

This edition published by arrangement with Harlequin Books S.A.

® and TM are trademarks of Harlequin Books S.A., used under license. Trademarks indicated with ® are registered in the United States Patent and Trademark Office, the Canadian Trade Marks Office and in other countries.

Visit Silhouette at www.eHarlequin.com

Printed in U.S.A.

Books by Judith Lyons

Silhouette Special Edition

Awakened by His Kiss #1296
Lt. Kent: Lone Wolf #1398
The Man in Charge #1462
Alaskan Nights #1547

JUDITH LYONS

lives in the deep woods in Wisconsin, where anyone who is familiar with the area will tell you one simply cannot survive the bitter winters without a comfortable chair, a cozy fireplace and a stack of good reading. When she decided winters were too cold for training horses and perfect for writing what she loved to read most— romance novels—she put pen to paper and delved into the exciting world of words and phrases and, most important of all, love and romance. Judith loves to hear from her readers. You can contact her through her Web site at http://www.judithlyons.com.

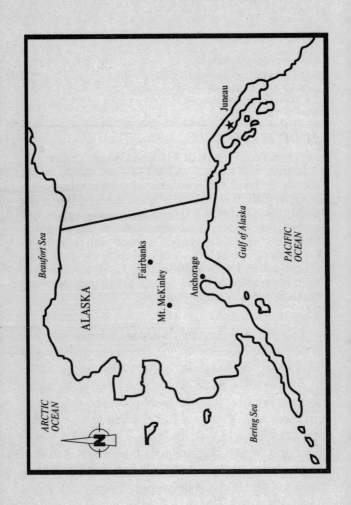

Chapter One

Fire in the cockpit.

Fear pounded through Winnie Mae Taylor like a squadron of F-16s on attack, coating her skin in a cold sweat and cramming her heart into her throat.

Another blue flame flicked out from under the dash, licked over the instrument panel and then disappeared again. The tiny flames came and went so quickly she might have thought the blue flicker was a figment of her imagination, but the steady curl of smoke streaming from under the dash and filling the cabin of the small, single-engine plane was all too real.

"Winnie! Get this plane turned around. We've

got to get back to the airport.'' Bob Smith, her passenger, snapped the sharp command.

Winnie strangled the smooth plastic of the yoke. With his black, wavy hair, tanned skin, and the beard shadow covering his square jawline, Bob Smith reminded her of a panther. Handsome. Strong. Alluring. He even moved like the black predator. Controlled. Fluid. All leashed power and natural grace.

His presence filled the cabin of the small plane. His heat poured into her right shoulder. And his raw maleness charged the atmosphere, making her nerves hum and her stomach churn and frustration pound in her brain.

She should have followed her instincts in the lobby this morning and run the minute she'd seen the man. One glance had been enough to tell her Bob Smith was the type of man who reminded any woman within a city block that she wasn't just a female—she was a woman. And the last thing Winnie needed was that kind of reminder.

After her ex-husband's crushing betrayal, she'd come to Alaska to start a new life. An independent life. A life *without* men. Unfortunately, running hadn't been an option this morning, and it wasn't an option now. Like it or not she and Smith were in this together.

Pushing herself into action, she snapped the main switch off, killing all electricity to her instrument panel. If the fire was under the dash, it was electrical. She didn't need to feed the flames. And the engine and propeller created their own electricity.

She pitched her voice above the loud whine of the engine. "Forget the airport. We need to start looking for a place to set down. Now."

Smith's dark brown eyes fixed on her like a pair of lasers. "You sure it's that bad? We're a long way from nowhere."

Didn't she know it. But she'd thought through every lousy option. The fire wasn't at a critical point yet. It was still small, more smoldering circuits than leaping flames at this stage of the game. But with fuel lines riddling the front of the cockpit, it would be foolish to make a run for the small airport they'd flown out of. "We're not waiting for it to get that bad. We're setting down now. Help me find a hole in these trees."

He stared at her unwaveringly as he wondered, no doubt, if she was making an intelligent, thought-out decision or just panicking.

She met his gaze squarely. "It's a rational decision, Smith. Help me pull it off."

He held her gaze another long second, then he gave his head a short, quick nod. "One emergency landing strip coming up." He turned to his window, beginning his search for an open stretch of land.

A small thread of relief slid through her. Getting them down in one piece was going to be hard enough without her passenger fighting her on every decision. And it felt good to have Smith on her side.

There was something about the man—an air of

danger, of confidence—that made her think he'd been in tight situations before. And if he was confident she could get them down, maybe they *were* going to squeak out of this ugly situation.

Tears running from her eyes from the smoke, she turned to look out her own window, searching desperately for a clear space in the landscape below. There had to be an open space down there. *There had to be.*

But only the dark green tops of pines stared back at her as the noxious smoke filled her lungs, sending her into a coughing fit. "Open your window," she hollered, her voice rough from the caustic fumes.

Smith leaned toward her, his shoulder brushing hers, his brown eyes leaking tears from the smoke just like hers. "Won't the fresh oxygen feed the fire?"

"We'll have to risk it. I can't land blind. Or unconscious. The only thing burning under that dash is plastic. And it's loaded with cyanide. Open your window."

With another succinct nod he turned the latch on his window and pushed the bottom open.

She followed suit. Fresh air rushed into the plane, sending the dingy smoke into a frantic swirl that momentarily blinded her. But once the air currents established themselves they pulled the smoke out of the plane.

She sucked in the fresh air. Smoke and fumes still burned her throat, but she could breathe without coughing. And she could see the ground more clearly now. Unfortunately, the only thing coming into view was a mountainside of pines. Not so much as a pinhole of terra firma peeked through the dark green tops. "You see anything over there?"

"There's a small space off to my right."

She didn't like the word *small,* but with nothing on her side she might settle. Urgency pounding at her temples, she snapped the plane over, tipping the wings steeply so she could look out his window. Following his pointed finger, she spotted the opening immediately. Frustration poured through her. "It's not big enough."

"How big a space do we need?"

She drew in a breath to holler, coughed, then tried again. "I need at least fourteen hundred feet. Eighteen hundred would be better. That way we can fly back out if we douse the fire before it causes major damage." Not that she had much hope of that. But thinking ahead is what flying was all about.

"I got nothing here."

"Keep looking. I'm going to fly over the peak. The whole other side of the mountain will open up for us once we're over." And she prayed to God there wasn't a tree on it. They glided over the top.

Nothing but a sea of dark green pines.

Her heart pounded harder. She glanced at the dash. Flames danced constantly with the smoky tendrils now, licking over the instrument panel like blue devils' tongues. Frustration flooded her. She should have stuck to her guns and refused to take this charter. In her determination to live a quiet, independent life she'd hired on at Henry's to fly cargo, *not* charters.

But with one of Henry's pilots in the hospital and the other one celebrating his first anniversary, she'd been the only pilot on duty. And when Henry had shot her that I've-got-a-paying-customer-waiting-in-the-lobby-and-two-boys-to-put-through-college look, she'd caved in and agreed to take the panther to his destination.

And now they both might pay dearly for that decision.

"There." Smith pointed off to the right.

Hope surging through her, she snapped the plane over again, praying this site would be big enough. Close enough. Close was important now. The flames were getting bigger by the second, the blue tongues reaching toward the small instrument box sitting directly under the dash between her and Smith's seat.

She followed Smith's finger to a big open field. It was big enough. But… "It's too far. We need something closer." Panic squeezed the air from her lungs.

"Are you sure? Did you see the cabin? There might be people there. Certainly there's shelter."

She shook her head, wishing to God she wasn't sure. "It's too far. We'll never make it." She was beginning to wonder if they were going to make it at all. Even with the windows open the smoke was getting heavier. Much longer and she wouldn't be able to see to land. And the blue flames flicked steadily closer to the instrument box between their feet.

She leveled the wings, railing at the fates and staring at the ground below her. *Come on, give me a break. All I'm asking for is a few hundred feet of ground, not a parting of the sea.*

And then she saw it. A small tear-shaped clearing. It wasn't long enough. Any way she played it she was going to hit the trees at the end. But if she clipped the top of the trees on her approach, got the plane on the ground as early as possible, used full flaps and stood on the brakes, she could soften the impact. Barring the thousands of things that could go wrong with that scenario, they might walk away.

She banked the wings and lined up for approach, her palms slick and clammy. "That's our spot. We're going in."

Smith let out an ugly curse. "Can you put this thing down in that small a space? It's not much bigger than the one I pointed out earlier."

"We're out of choices."

"We'll never be able to fly back out."

She spared him a quick glance. "The least of our problems."

His eyes snapped to hers. "What's our biggest?"

"See that?" She pointed to the small instrument box between their seats. The blue flames were almost long enough to reach now, their deadly tongues flicking hungrily toward the floor.

"Yeah."

"That's our fuel line."

* * *

Son of a *bitch*. Impotent rage poured through Rand Michaels, aka Bob Smith. He was barely into the mission and it was already going sour. But there wasn't a damned thing he could do about it except push Winnie to use every ounce of the aviation skill she possessed to get them on the ground. And if the report he'd read on her aerobatic act meant anything, she had plenty of skill.

He pinned her with a not-only-do-I-know-you-can-do-it-but-I-damned-well-expect-you-to-do-it glare he'd learned from an army sergeant who could make men walk on water. "I don't care how you do it. Just do it. You get this plane on the ground in one piece."

Her lips tightened and her eyes crackled at the command. "One piece isn't going to happen. Pray for us getting on the ground and out before it turns into a giant ball of fire."

"Just get it done." She wasn't going to die on his watch, dammit. He couldn't stand one more death on his hands.

His gut twisted. He was so tired of this game. So tired of pulling people into his web only to discover too late that they were innocent. That they had no business in his deadly trap.

Of course, he didn't know if Winnie was innocent.

But he didn't know she was guilty, either. And the trap wasn't supposed to have been deadly. His mission here was simply to insinuate himself into

Winnie Mae Taylor's life and find out what she knew about her husband's disappearance with fifty million of Uncle Sam's dollars. Find out if she was involved in the scheme. Discover if her divorce from Tucker Taylor and her sudden move to Alaska were merely the actions of an innocent or the move of a woman trying to throw the government off her husband's scent. But a simple plane ride had changed from easy to life threatening in a single heartbeat.

Frustration clawing at his gut, he turned back to his window—and almost had a heart attack. She had the plane headed straight for a tree. "Watch out—"

A hard thump shook the plane as it plowed through the top of the pine.

Winnie's hand tightened on the yoke as the jolt of the impact reverberated through her. "It's okay. I did it on purpose. Hang on." Her lips getting thinner by the second, she pushed the plane ever downward.

The wheels hit the ground hard, bounced twice and then careered over the rough, uneven turf. Rand's heart pounded as the stand of trees at the end of the field rushed at them at an alarming clip. But Winnie seemed to be in control. Leaning forward, she threw a lever and tromped both feet on the brakes, pressing them down with all her strength.

The plane jerked back, its speed diminishing abruptly.

But it wasn't going to be enough.

They were going to eat those trees. The only

question was, how many of them? He grabbed the door handle and shoved his feet against the floor.

The plane slammed into the pines. Metal crumpled. Wings collapsed. The sound of crunching timber and tearing metal filled the air. Finally the plane came to a hard, bone-racking halt.

The seat belt practically cut him in two as it kept him from being thrown through the windshield, but when he snapped back against the seat, he was still in one piece. He glanced at Winnie through the rapidly building cloud of smoke. She looked a little stunned but unhurt. Thank God. But the relief had barely registered when his nose twitched. He drew in a deeper breath.

Gas.

Adrenaline launched him into action. "Out. *Now.*"

Part of the wing on Winnie's side of the plane thrust through her window, its jagged edges slashing into the plane like giant sharks' teeth. She wasn't getting out that door.

He flipped his seat belt open with one hand, jerked his door handle up with the other and gave the door a shove, but it barely budged.

Urgency clawing at his hide, he turned in his seat and leveled both feet at his door. He kicked with all his strength, ignoring the heat from the flames snapping at his back. He had to get her out of this plane. Now.

Finally the door gave way. "We're out." Grabbing Winnie's wrist, he jumped from the plane, dragging her behind him.

Her feet hit the ground right behind his, but then she pulled out of his grasp. "Wait! There's survival gear in the back of the plane. We'll need it."

"Screw the gear. It's gonna blow." He snatched her wrist again, pulling her from the plane.

She dug in and tried to jerk out of his grip. "We have to have that gear. Without it we'll never make it. Not in Alaska."

No time to argue. "Then I'll get it. You get away from the damned plane." He had to get her out of here. He turned her toward the open field and gave her a good shove. "Go." Ignoring the strong scent of gas and the vivid image of his body barbecued to a crisp, he spun back to the mangled aircraft and slammed the cargo door open.

Leaning inside, he spotted the gear immediately. It was neatly tied up in cargo nets strapped to the side of the plane. Reaching in, he struggled with the stubborn knots keeping the nets up, the smoke growing thicker, the flames bigger, the pounding of his heart harder. Who the hell had tied these things in the first place?

Suddenly a feminine body leaned in, pressing against him, reaching over his hands. "No. Like this." Winnie's fingers grabbed a single tie, yanked, and the whole net fell away.

"Dammit, get out of here!"

"I will, but..." She lunged across the plane toward the cargo net behind her seat. "I need this box.'' Her quick fingers pulled the net open and snatched a gold-foil box about the size of a small toaster from the green netting.

Anger surged through him like a ballistic missile. He dropped the survival gear, grabbed hold of her waist and jerked her out of the plane. ''Go!'' His voice thundered around them as he shoved her away from the plane for the second time.

To his great surprise and imminent relief she started running as soon as her feet hit the ground, the package wrapped tightly in her arms. He snatched the survival gear and his rifle from under the seat and followed hard on her heels.

Fifteen steps beyond the plane's tail, the explosion knocked them to the ground, the blast exploding in their ears. A wave of heat raced over them, and then there was nothing but the roar of fire.

He scrambled to his feet, snatched his rifle with one hand, grabbed Winnie's wrist with the other and dragged her with him. When the flames no longer scorched them, he dropped the gear to the ground and let go of Winnie.

She went to her knees, clutching the gold-foil box tight against her chest.

He scowled at the shiny gold cube with its wide gold ribbon and enormous, matching bow. ''What the hell is in that box worth risking your life for?''

''It's just—'' she looked away from him, a hint of pink coloring her cheeks ''—a present.''

His senses snapped to attention at her hesitation and blush. Whatever was in that box, he didn't think it was *just* a present. It was either a very important present…or something else altogether. Money? Her share of the fifty mil? Papers leading to a Swiss bank account—and Tucker?

Maybe. God knew he'd seen stranger things in this business than a person carrying around a box full of cash or important papers they were afraid of losing. Especially if those papers pointed to their guilt in a crime.

But discovering what was in the box would have to wait. Winnie was looking the worse for wear. The flush had already faded. She was as pale as the proverbial ghost, and her breathing was shallow and uneven.

He knelt beside her. "You all right?"

She gave a determined but unconvincing nod and set the box down with shaky hands. Very, very shaky hands. Then she looked back to him with a guarded expression. "Don't touch it."

He held his hands up. "Fine." With the Alaskan wilderness around them and their plane going up in smoke, he had a feeling there would be plenty of time to delve into the mysteries of the box. And at this moment his only concern was Winnie's well-being. He didn't like her pallor one bit. "Are you sure you're not hurt?"

She shook her head. "No. Just…"

Scared out of her wits. He knew the feeling. The adrenaline was still pumping through his own veins. "You did a good job with the plane," he reassured her, trying to push her toward the realization that the point of danger was past.

She ran a shaky hand through her hair, her gaze going to the burning hulk behind them, her lips twisting wryly. "Yeah, peachy."

A hint of a smile pulled at his lips. Innocent or guilty, she was a gutsy thing. Gutsy...and pretty.

He shoved the thought away. This was not the time to be thinking how pretty she was, even now, kneeling on the ground disheveled and upset. Not the time to be thinking how good she'd felt pressed up against him as she'd leaned into the plane to untie the nets. Not the time to be thinking how long it had been since he'd been around anything as soft and lovely as Winnie Mae Taylor.

But it was hard to take his eyes off the delicate lines of her face and the long, black curls cascading to her waist. Even in wild disarray her hair was beautiful. Shiny and lush...and, man, he wanted to reach out and stroke the riotous strands. See if they were as soft as they looked.

But since he was here to discover if the lady was involved in anything illegal—and send her to prison if she was—he squelched the urge and stuck to the task at hand. He ran his gaze over her, making sure she was all right.

And that's when he saw the blood starting to soak the sleeve of her left arm. Damn. He leaned forward, grasping her elbow. "You *are* hurt."

She glanced at her arm, her complexion blanching even more as she saw the blood. Panic flashed in her green eyes. But she didn't give in to it. Gritting her teeth, she pulled away from him. "I can get it." Drawing a ragged, determined breath, she pulled the edges of the torn sleeve apart and tried to look at the wound.

He gritted his teeth as she struggled with the hole in her sleeve. Between her angle of sight and the uncooperative material, she couldn't be seeing a damned thing. "Oh, for crying out loud." He crawled over to her and brushed her hand aside. "Let me look."

Obviously, the rapidly reddening sleeve had convinced her she might need a little help, after all, because she didn't protest as he pulled the tear apart and peered in. Unfortunately, he couldn't see much through the small hole, either. Taking hold of the material on either side of the tear, he ripped the sleeve open. His stomach twisted as the gaping wound came into view.

Damn, damn, *damn*.

Four inches long and plenty deep, the bleeding gash glared back at him. Guilt poured through him. If he hadn't lied to her about who he was, if he'd just told her straight out that he was an agent for the government, and he wanted to know if she knew where her husband was, none of this would have happened.

But he hadn't done that. He'd come into this mission the same way he'd gone into every other mission for the past eight years. Undercover. As a Judas. Because in the long run being a Judas—

working his way into his target's life, into his or her trust—was the quickest way to elicit information if the target was working outside the law.

If.

The word stuck in his craw like a double-edged sword as he stared at Winnie's torn flesh and gushing blood.

If.

Chapter Two

Winnie looked away from the bleeding slash and tried to ignore the pain as Smith poked and prodded. "This isn't good."

Smith grimaced. "Don't panic. It's ugly but not fatal."

Ugly didn't cover it. Now that the adrenaline had slowed to a trickle, her arm was beginning to throb. It burned as voraciously as the plane. Even more frightening was the realization that the nasty cut was the least of her worries.

Smith's heat soaked into her, sending shivers along her already frayed nerves. She was stuck in the middle of nowhere with a man that affected her far more than could possibly be good for a woman who'd decided to live a solitary, independent life. *And* although she'd managed to get them on the ground in one piece, it was now her duty to get them—get Smith—safely back to civilization.

She stared at the plane, fear sliding over her. Henry had said everything a pilot would need to stay alive was in the bundle Smith had pulled out of the plane. But she didn't know how to use any of it. And the Alaskan wild was no place for tenderfoots.

Too many dangers waited for the unsuspecting and naive. Hazardous terrain, plummeting temperatures and *lots* of roving, carnivorous wildlife. Big cats, packs of wolves…and bears.

Grizzly bears.

Oh, God. The first week she'd been in Alaska, a grizzly had tried to claw his way into her cabin. Being awakened by the sound of tearing wood and the beast's angry growls had scared her to death. And the deep, slashing claw marks she'd found on her door the next morning had done nothing to alleviate that fear. Her heart raced. How would she ever protect herself and Smith from that?

She winced as he tore her sleeve off so he could get to the cut unimpeded. "I don't know how to break this to you, Mr. Smith, but we're stuck in the middle of nowhere with nothing but our feet to get us from point A to point B—and we're a long, long way from point B."

"I'll tell you what, let's worry about that after we get this arm fixed up, okay?" Though his tone was even and controlled, a current of urgency ran under his words that made her glance down at her arm.

Blood. Lots and lots of blood now. Flowing down her exposed arm to her fingertips and dripping into the patchy grass. A wave of dizziness hit her. She swayed on her knees, darkness closing in on her from the edges of her vision.

Big hands, warm and strong, grabbed her shoulders. "Easy. Let's get you sitting down." He resettled her into a sitting position and gave her a moment to steady herself. "Okay?"

Not by a long shot. She'd been struggling to piece her life back together after her ex, Tucker, had shattered it to pieces. Now she could feel what little she'd pieced back together crumbling around her. But as the person in charge of this fiasco, succumbing to the darkness wasn't an option.

She drew a deep, steadying breath and pushed the encroaching blackness away. "I'm fine."

He watched her closely, as if he didn't quite believe her words and would make his own decision about how okay she was. Slowly he let go of her shoulders, making sure she stayed up as he did so. "If you get dizzy again, lean forward and put your head down. Got it?"

She nodded. "Got it."

He quickly folded the bloody sleeve he'd just pulled from her arm into a small pad and pressed it to her cut.

She hissed as the pain exploded in her arm, tears stinging her eyes.

He grimaced but didn't ease up on the pressure. "Sorry. But we've got to get this bleeding stopped. Do you have a first-aid kit in that bundle of gear you made us haul out of the plane?"

She managed a nod. "In the big outside pocket on the left."

"Good." He clasped her hand and pressed it hard on top of the square of plaid flannel. "Hold this tight while I get the kit." He scrambled up and jogged to the bundle of gear near the tail of the plane.

She watched his progress. He moved in a smooth, economic manner that showed competence and confidence and a pure male power that was impossible to ignore. Watching him, it was easy to see that he was completely at home in emergency situations.

It was also easy to see by the way he'd questioned her decisions in the plane and the way he'd taken over once they hit the ground that he was used to being in charge. That he was *good* at being in charge. And with her shoulder burning and exhaustion swamping her it would be easy to let him take over. Let him take care of her. But...

She was in charge of her life now. And just because she was hurting wasn't an excuse to get weak-kneed. In fact, getting weak-kneed about a man as compelling as Smith when she knew from vast experience that most men were *not* the trustworthy, upstanding citizens they portrayed would be extremely unwise.

She looked down at the bloody sleeve she held to her arm. Torn flesh and blood. Bear bait if she'd ever seen it. Her heart pounded in her chest. "Hurry up, Smith. We've got to get this blood cleaned up before we start attracting the local wildlife."

The first-aid kit in hand, he jogged back to her. "Don't worry about the wildlife. I grabbed my rifle on the way out, remember?" He tipped his head toward where he'd dropped it, not six feet from where she sat.

She hadn't noticed he'd carried his rifle out during those frantic moments. But the important thing wasn't that he'd brought it—there was one in her gear—the important thing was: "Do you know how to use it?"

His brows snapped together as he dropped down beside her and opened the first-aid kit. "Why would I be carrying the damned thing if I didn't?"

She bit her lower lip, heat flushing her cheeks. "I have one in my survival gear—it's required by the FAA—but I don't know how to use it."

He looked up from his perusal of the medical supplies, a single brow cocked in disbelief. "The FAA requires you to carry a rifle, but doesn't require that you learn how to use it?"

She nodded.

Shaking his head, he got busy cleaning up her arm. "I won't comment on the idiocy of that. Hang on, this is going to sting."

She reflexively tried to jerk away as he cleaned her cut with alcohol-soaked gauze. But he held on firmly, working quickly, gently. She closed her eyes against the pain and tried not to think about the half dozen bears that might already be tracking them down even as Smith worked. But she couldn't keep the thought at bay. "Are you any good with it?"

His forehead crinkled in question. "With what?"

"The rifle."

He glanced up just long enough to spare her an amused smile. "I can hit the broad side of a barn."

"How about a bear?" Despite her efforts to keep it out, worry laced her words.

His hand stilled and he looked up, his brown eyes studying her. "Are you afraid of bears?"

"I'm not *afraid* of bears," she quickly clarified. "I just don't like them."

That little smile got a bit wider. "Uh-huh."

All right, she wasn't fooling him. But she was doing the best she could. She was a pilot for pity's sake. Not Daniel Boone.

He looked up again, his expression surprisingly gentle. "Don't worry about the bears. I won't let one get you. I'm good with the rifle."

Surprise shimmered through her. No one had ever offered to protect her before. Her father had never been around when she was a kid to chase the monsters from under the bed or out from the closet. And Tucker had always been too busy saving the world to be concerned with her little corner of the universe. It was nice having someone worry about her. Comforting and—

Enough. It was fine if she wanted to let Smith shoot the bears. She obviously wasn't going to be doing it herself. But this warm and fuzzy feeling…

Ridiculous. Dangerous. She *knew* men were much more likely to deliver treachery than come through on their promises. And just because Smith was handsome and strong and...all right...sexy, didn't mean he was any different.

But still... She tipped her head. "Thank you."

He shrugged, holding up a pressure bandage. "No problem. Now I need you to hold your arm still and push against me while I wrap this on tight, okay? It's gonna hurt, but I need you to bite the bullet. Got it?" Regret filled his gaze. He obviously didn't want to hurt her, but he knew as well as she that there was no way around it.

She gritted her teeth. "Go."

With a grimace of his own he placed the heavy pad of the bandage over the gash, pulled the elastic bandage attached to it tight around her arm and secured it with the metal clips. "Done."

Pain swamped her and darkness clouded the edges of her vision again. Closing her eyes, she held her breath, willing the pain to subside.

Smith's hands found her shoulders again, holding her up. Comforting her. "Easy does it. Breathe deep." His warm breath whispered over her cheek.

That warm, fuzzy feeling slid through her again, but she studiously ignored it as she waited for the pain to back off. Finally she was able to draw a shaky breath. And then another.

Smith's hands eased up. "Okay?"

She opened her eyes and eased out of his grip.

Relying on those warm, strong arms could not possibly be the smart thing to do. "Yeah. Fine."

"Okay, let's get you cleaned up then." He started cleaning the blood from the lower part of her arm with fresh gauze.

Centering her own concentration on the problem at hand, she looked at the plane. Another five minutes and there would be nothing but a charred, smoking frame. Panic reared its ugly head again. She knew from every report she'd read on downed planes in Alaska it could be days before another plane flew over this area and spotted the wreck.

Weeks.

Some crash sights were never found.

Lord, she had to get them someplace safe. But where? She suddenly remembered the field Smith had pointed out earlier. "The cabin."

Smith looked up, tossed the pad he'd used to clean her arm and grabbed another. "What?"

Urgency pounded through her. "That cabin by the field you spotted earlier. We have to get there."

"Why?"

"Because somebody with a radio and transportation who can get us out of here might be there. At the very least the cabin will give us shelter."

And they *needed* shelter. Against the elements. Against the bears. "It's a bit of a hike. But we can make it. I took a compass reading on it when we were in the air. And if that bundle of gear was packed with survival in mind, there has to be a compass in it.'' She started to get up, urgency pushing the pain and shock away.

Smith grasped her arm. "Whoa. I'm not done yet." Gently, but firmly, he pulled her back down. "You go traipsing through the woods with blood all over your arm, you *will* attract the bears. And we're not going anywhere for at least an hour. I want you to rest—"

"An hour!" Dread closed in on her like a black cloud. "No way. That cabin is two ridges over. We're going to need every minute to make it there before nightfall."

Smith just shook his head, his grip keeping her from going anywhere. "Right now your blood's running through your system like a freight train, which is why you're bleeding so hard. Hiking will only make it worse. You need to stay still, rest, give your blood time to coagulate."

She shook her head, trying to pull from his grip. "I'll be fine."

His fingers tightened on her arm, his expression as unyielding as the granite mountain behind him. "An hour, Winnie."

If she thought her life had been a shambles before this flight, she couldn't begin to imagine how much worse it would be if something happened to Smith out here while he was under her care. Besides, the sooner she got Smith back to his life and she got back to hers, the better. "No. Now. We *have* to get to that cabin before dark."

His brown-eyed gaze bore into hers, his grasp still tight on her arm.

She stared back with stubborn determination.

His lips thinned into a narrow line, but he must have realized she wasn't going to take no for an answer because he finally released her arm. He didn't get up and prepare to leave though. He planted himself on the ground, kicked his legs out in front of him, crossed them at the ankle and leaned back on his hands as if he were settling in for an afternoon of cloud gazing. "If you want to go to the cabin. Go. But I'm not going anywhere. Not for an hour."

Anger and frustration pounded through her. "Mr. Smith, I think you're probably used to being in charge. But when a charter plane goes down in the bush the person in charge of getting the passengers back to civilization safe and sound is the *pilot*. And on this expedition that's me."

He stared back at her, one shoulder dipping in a careless shrug. "You're not going to save us by leaving a blood trail for the bears to follow. Or by passing out because you've lost half your blood. So pull up a rock, put your butt on it and give your blood time to slow down."

She clenched her hands, impotence pouring through her. "You're not going to budge, are you?"

He shook his head, a hint of humor pulling at his lips.

With an angry growl she lowered herself to the ground opposite him and shot him her darkest scowl.

"Fine, you win. This time. But I just want you to know that I'm trying to start a new life here. One that will be a lot better than the one I left behind, if things work out. And if you goof that up for me by getting one, or both of us, eaten by bears, I'm going to be one unhappy camper."

Chapter Three

Rand inhaled the scent of pine, keeping a close eye on Winnie as she made her way between the tall pines and up the next incline ahead of him. Earlier in the trek, determined to get to the cabin, she'd groused at him for constantly looking back on her to make sure she was all right, so he'd taken the flank position on the trail. Back here he could keep an eye on her without raising her ire.

And if the scenery—her soft curls swinging against the narrow line of her waist and her curvy little backside—made the hike more enjoyable than he had any right to hope it would be, well, he'd live with the guilt.

Unfortunately, the guilt he was accumulating with

her relentless push to the cabin would be a little harder to shoulder. She was tired and worn, but she pushed herself on unceasingly to get them—him—to the cabin before dark.

He'd made her stop and rest twice. Rests that had made her growl and grit her teeth, but when he'd planted his butt, she'd seen the futility of going on without him and followed suit. But she hadn't liked it.

Not that those breaks were up for negotiation. They weren't. He didn't give a damn if they made it to the cabin or not. He'd worked his first undercover mission in his early twenties. He'd spent 130 days in the Central American jungle infiltrating a rebel army to discover their plans to overthrow the local government. And he'd worked a thousand missions just like it since, first as a CIA operative and later as a mercenary with his current employer, Freedom Rings. Which meant he'd spent most of his adult life camping out somewhere. Camping out where the prospect of an enemy attack would come from a source much more deadly than a few grumpy bears.

But Winnie wasn't a soldier. She was a civilian. He could understand why she wanted to get to the cabin. She would feel safer with four walls around her. Most people did.

And if it would make her relax a little to be at the cabin, he was happy to indulge her need. Providing she didn't hurt herself getting there. But he didn't like her pushing herself so hard for him, didn't like her thinking she was responsible for his safety. It was too...sweet. The last thing he deserved was her sweetness. Anyone's sweetness. But more than that, her concern made her seem too innocent.

And he didn't want her to be innocent.

If he was going to drag her through this nightmare, he wanted her to be guilty. Because if she'd helped Tucker plan the theft, he could walk away knowing she'd brought this misery on herself. But if she was innocent...

He stepped over a rock, cursing the fates for sticking him in the middle of this mess. If the CIA had just called on some other agency instead of Freedom Rings to help with their little arms sting involving the drug lord in Colombia, some other poor bastard would be here now, trying to dig the truth out of Winnie.

But the Agency hadn't called anyone else. They'd called their favorite dog of clandestine wars, Griffon Tyner, because they knew he was competent and honest. And they knew Rand worked for him. They knew they could plug Rand into the CIA-directed mission with little fuss or muss. So he'd been the one caught with his pants down when the fifty mil had disappeared.

Rand grimaced as he followed Winnie up another small incline. He'd had a bad feeling about the assignment from the moment he'd met the CIA agent in charge of the mission—Winnie's ex, Tucker Taylor. The man had been too cocky, too smug and too damned slick, with his blond, angelic looks and saintly smile. All those white teeth had made Rand wonder what the man was up to.

And the lowly bastard had been up to something all right. Unfortunately, Rand had discovered too late what that something was. So here he was in Alaska, following an injured woman—a beautiful, sweet woman from what he could see—through the woods and praying to God he found her guilty of a crime that would send her to jail for a good portion of her natural life just so his conscience could be clear about the hell he was putting her through now.

He was as lowly a bastard as Taylor.

Ahead of him, Winnie's feet slipped on the loose dirt. She kept herself from landing on her butt by catching herself with her injured arm—the only arm free since she was carrying her precious box with her good arm. A sharp groan rolled down the trail.

Dammit. He lengthened his stride, catching up with her. "You okay?"

She managed a small nod as she righted herself and walked on. "Yeah, fine."

But she didn't look fine. Her complexion was blanched with pain as she continued up the mountain. Keeping pace with her, he stared at the offending gold box with its hideous bow. "You shouldn't be carrying that thing. If it's too damned important to leave behind *I* should be carrying it."

She looked at the ground, embarrassment flushing her cheeks again, but she didn't say anything. She obviously wasn't letting the box out of her hands, and she wasn't going to waste her breath fighting about it.

He ran an agitated hand through his hair. He wanted this charade over. And with her watchdog-like care of that damned box—and the color that hit her cheeks every time he mentioned it—he was leaning more and more toward the opinion that the answers he needed were covered in gold foil.

He narrowed his eyes on the shiny cube. "I don't know what could possibly be so important you had to carry that box halfway across Alaska. Whatever is in there can't possibly be so expensive you couldn't replace it if you had to."

Her gaze flitted away. "Maybe it has nothing to do with how much it cost. Maybe it's something irreplaceable. Or sentimental. Like an heirloom."

He stared at her profile. Beautiful. Stubborn. Guilty? "Is it?"

She was obviously hiding something, but when she looked back to him, her chin was raised stubbornly and her eyes sparkled with cool determination. "It doesn't matter. I'm not leaving it behind, Mr. Smith. It's important."

Obviously. The question was, Why was it important? Did it hold the key to the fifty mil?

He switched his gaze back to the box. Maybe the easiest way to solve this case was to look in the damned thing after she went to sleep tonight. It wouldn't be that hard. It wasn't wrapped. It was just a gold-foil gift box with a ribbon tied around it.

Definitely an option he would give serious

thought to if rescue wasn't waiting for them. But right now he needed to pay attention to the climb up the ridge. The mountain's pitch was getting steeper. The ground looser.

As if to prove his observation, Winnie slipped on the loose ground again. But this time she couldn't catch herself. Her feet went out from under her, sending her sprawling. She landed with a hard thump, her precious box flying into the air. The gold cube flew apart and came down in a hailstorm of pieces.

Damn. He rushed the few steps to her and squatted down beside her. "You all right?" No fresh blood seeped through the bandage, and now that the shock of the fall was over, no real pain registered on her expression.

She nodded on a frustrated sigh. "I'm fine, but..." She waved a hand at the debris around her.

Triumph surged through him. For once in this screwed-up mission fate was taking his side. Smiling grimly, he quickly looked around at the box's scattered contents.

But his triumph died a quick and painful death.

There were no papers strewn around them. No small- or large-denomination bills. Just...makeup. Makeup and several bottles filled with all the stuff women used on their faces. His gut clenched.

He snatched up one of the small, clear compacts filled with a colored powder and held it up in disgust. "You risked your life back at the plane for fifteen dollars worth of *makeup?*"

Indignation sparked in her eyes as she snatched the small case from his fingers. "It's not fifteen dollars worth. It's *eighty* dollars worth. And—"

"So you risked your life for *eighty* bucks?" He wanted to strangle her. But he had the sinking feeling he'd already caused her far more grief than she deserved. He dropped down beside her and plowed his fingers through his hair.

She grabbed up the slightly battered box and began picking up the makeup, carefully wiping it clean and placing it back in the box, piece by piece. "Eighty bucks might not be much to a man who can afford to charter a plane. But it's a lot to me." Fresh color flooded her cheeks.

That's what her blushes had been about? Not guilt, but embarrassment at her financial status? He shook his head, acid pouring into his gut. She'd risked her life for eighty dollars worth of makeup because she feared she wouldn't be able to remake the money anytime soon?

He shoved himself to his feet and strode away, that sinking feeling all but drowning him. *Dammit.* Damn this screwed-up world and this soul-eating job. And damn *him.* He'd dragged her through a plane crash, over what seemed like half of the Alaskan state, and for what?

Nothing. Not a damned thing.

No woman dove into a burning plane to save a gift worth eighty lousy dollars and then carried it halfway across Alaska with a throbbing arm if she believed her husband was coming back for her with fifty million dollars. No way. No how.

Beautiful, sweet Winnie Mae Taylor…was innocent.

Humiliation heated Winnie's cheeks. She hated admitting how poor she was. Silly. She'd never defined people by their wealth before. Why she would start now she didn't know.

Well, actually, she did know. But she hated admitting it.

She was embarrassed to find herself so poor because that would mean admitting to others—to herself—*why* she was broke. She'd have to admit that Tucker Taylor had left her high and dry. That somewhere in the past four years he'd stopped loving her. That perhaps he had *never* really loved her.

A cold, painful laugh echoed through her head. What was it about her that drove the important men in her life away? Was she lacking something? Was there something about her that simply made her unlovable? Or were men just basically lying, cheating scoundrels put here on earth to complicate every woman's life?

She sighed, swiping at an errant tear. It was an old, tired mystery. One she'd been grappling with since she was a little girl trying to figure out why her father thought it was okay to wander back into her and her mother's life just often enough to keep his place in their hearts. And why he thought it was okay to clean their bank account out and leave them destitute every time he decided he needed to leave again.

She drew a watery breath and shook her head, carefully wiping the dirt from the shiny gold tube before dropping it into the slightly damaged box with the other goodies. Stupid. Now was hardly the time to be sitting around feeling sorry for herself. She was in the middle of God knew where with her arm aching like the very devil, bears on their trail and night closing in fast. She wiped away the tears stinging her eyes and hastened her makeup retrieval. The cabin was still a good hour away. They needed to get a move on.

Smith's boots came into view and then he was kneeling beside her. "Let me help." He picked up a small compact of light-pink blush and wiped it against his faded jeans to clean it.

She didn't want him close enough to see the sheen of tears in her eyes. She shook her head, taking the makeup from his fingers. "I'm fine. I can get it."

"I know you can, but I want to help."

"Please…"

He sighed, picking up a bottle of face cleaner and wiping it off. "Look, I'm sorry if I embarrassed you." He dropped the bottle into the box, his lips pressed into a hard line. "I'm sorry about this whole damned mess."

She shook her head. "*You* don't have anything to apologize for. If anything *I* should be apologizing to you. If not for crashing the plane and almost killing you, then for sitting here sniffling like an idiot when I should be getting you to that cabin.''

He gave her a comforting smile. ''After the day you've had, you're entitled to the sniffling. As for the apologizing—'' His lips twisted into a grimace. ''It's the last thing you should be doing, trust me.''

She wondered briefly about the remark. But the events of the day and the pain in her arm were zapping her energy. If she didn't get off her knees and start moving, she feared she would be done for the day. She drew a deep, fortifying breath, dropped the last few items in the box and retied the fancy gold bow.

She looked at the end result with a shake of her head. ''A sad replica of the beautiful box the department store sent me out the door with, but it will have to do.''

Smith stared at the box, his brows pulled together unhappily. ''Whoever the gift is for ought to be glad to get it at all. Do you really think she would have wanted you to risk your life for it?''

That warm fuzzy feeling slid through her again.

Neither her father nor her ex would have given a second thought to her risking her life for anything. God knows her father had watched her do it at every air show they'd ever flown in. And pushed her to do more dangerous stunts with each appearance because the more dangerous the stunt the more money they could charge. And this stranger was worrying about her safety.

Lordy, she was at it again. She quickly squelched

the warm fuzzies. While she wanted to hope there were good guys in the world, she was all too aware they never seemed to fall into her path. And while Mr. Smith certainly seemed to be a bang-up guy, it didn't take a psychologist to know that three months after her ex's betrayal—and after this plane crash— she was just a wee bit vulnerable and undoubtedly not the best judge of character at the moment.

The last thing she needed to do was let some stranger, no matter how nice—or handsome—start playing with her emotions.

She was here to start an *independent* life.

And to that end, she needed to get them to that cabin, where, hopefully, someone with a radio powerful enough to call for help would be there to greet them.

Then she could get Mr. Smith on his way. And she could get on with building her new life. A life of solitude, where she wouldn't have to worry about men betraying her or treading on her heart.

Chapter Four

Rand strode beside Winnie, keeping a close eye on her, helping her up the trickier bits of terrain. Despite her spunk and her determination to get to the cabin, she was fast hitting the end of her endurance. Thankfully, their trek was almost over.

From the last, higher peak, they'd spotted the cabin not far down on the other side of this ridge. They'd been too far away to see if anyone was home, but they'd been able to choose the shortest path to their destination. Another ten minutes and they'd be there.

Just as well. Dusk had begun to settle. A nip had permeated the air, raising goose bumps on his skin.

He drew in a deep breath of the crisp, fresh air. God, it was beautiful here.

Rugged.

Wild.

Clean.

So damned clean. He drew in another breath, savoring the pine-laden crispness and drinking in the sight of the tall pines and the jagged rocks and the wild vegetation covering the ground. He couldn't remember the last time he'd been anywhere so... peaceful.

The hell holes he'd spent the past several years in while infiltrating everything from large bands of arms dealers to drug cartels had been anything but peaceful. Anything but clean. They'd been places where despair and desperation and seething, zealous anger had permeated the atmosphere, tainting the very air they breathed.

He drew in another cleansing breath and rubbed the chill from his arms. After the past six months of living in the jungles of South America, he wasn't used to the cooler temperatures. But he didn't mind them. As long as he could stay here in this pristine setting he wouldn't mind if it was forty below. Mind? Hell, he'd even revel in it if he could stay here and never face another undercover mission again.

But such wishful thinking was nothing more than...well, wishful thinking. He'd tried civilian life a few years back. It had been a dismal failure. Knowing how to ferret out someone's secrets only to call down the law enforcement agencies on their heads—agencies that usually carried big guns and left oceans of blood behind—wasn't a skill much needed in the real world. And he'd quickly realized he wasn't comfortable around normal people anymore. Decent people.

He'd found it was hard to relate to people when the only thing he could share was his most recent history. Go back much further than that, and he'd be explaining how he'd been responsible for the deaths of any number of men a month ago or a week ago.

True, most of those men were vicious guys who were making their money on the misery, sweat and death of others. Men who deserved to die. But for every arms dealer, every drug lord, every bad guy there were a dozen innocents—mothers, wives, children—who got caught in the action. It was those deaths that weighed on his soul. Those deaths that made him feel as if he were tainting the decent people of normal society. Those deaths that kept him firmly shackled to the mercenary life.

He grabbed Winnie's arm and helped her up a slippery piece of slope before she tried to make a go of it on her own and landed on her lovely, bruised backside again. "Come on, we're almost there."

A mountain of guilt pressed down on him as he watched her struggle against her pain and fatigue to make it up the few steps of incline. He knew that sometimes missions went bad. It wasn't anyone's fault. It was just one of those nasty little turns of life. But he didn't like it. And he never had been able to convince himself those turns weren't partly his fault.

Today wasn't any different.

So he'd live with the guilt. As he had a hundred times before. And he'd ignore the impulse to assuage it by telling her who he was. Because as much as he'd like to tell her he represented the CIA and that he was looking for her husband and the fifty million dollars the man had stolen and wash his hands of this whole ugly mess, it wasn't an option.

The first thing one learned in undercover work was that people were as unpredictable in their loyalties as a kite in the wind. While he was sure Tucker wasn't coming back to whisk Winnie off to a life of wealth and luxury, that's all he knew. He didn't know anything about the circumstances surrounding their divorce.

He had no idea whether Winnie would be willing to tell him secrets that would put dear old Tuck in prison. So he'd stay under cover, hang around her for the next few weeks, pretend to be her best bud so he could wheedle out of her whatever information she did have on her ex.

He hated the idea of betraying her, but there wasn't anything he could do about it. He could, however, do his best to make this awful day up to her. Not that he'd be able to completely atone, but he could damned well do *something*.

He helped her up another stretch of crumbling

rock. He didn't like her pallor or the tight line of her lips. Pain and fatigue were taking their toll. Two other things he couldn't do anything about. But he could distract her from them. He nodded at the box she still had tucked protectively into the crook of her elbow. "So tell me who the present's for."

She smiled. "Jenny Mallard, a young girl on my mail route. She's turning thirteen today."

The smile was definitely better than the grimace. "Teenager, huh? Big day. That's what the makeup's about, right? Welcome to young adulthood? I seem to remember my sisters getting piles of makeup on that birthday." He rolled his eyes. "And then they commandeered the bathroom and refused to give it up for *hours.*"

She chuckled softly. "Poor baby. And, yeah, I think makeup being given on a girl's thirteenth birthday is a pretty common tradition. I know that's when I got my first blush and lipstick from my mom." Her lips twisted unhappily. "Unfortunately, for Jenny, the tradition will have to wait for another day. Or so."

Great. Not only had he put this woman through hell, he'd deprived a little girl of her present. "The other girls at the party will give her makeup, though, right? My sisters got enough lipstick to last them their entire lives at their thirteenth birthday parties."

"Yeah, but there aren't any other girls going to Jenny's party. Jenny and her dad live out in the tundra. *Way* out in the tundra," she emphasized. "Where there are no roads and the nearest house is a good forty miles away. I was the only guest going. And that's because I have a plane."

"Won't Jenny's mom give her some? Surely the tradition won't get lost completely." He offered his hand so she could grab hold and pull herself up a big, sharp step.

Grabbing hold, she grimaced. "Jenny lost her mom three years ago to cancer."

Damn. He had to make this right. Somehow. "I'll tell you what, if someone's at the cabin when we get there, we'll get you home tonight, get you to a doc and into bed for a good sleep. Then tomorrow I'll charter another one of Henry's planes, and we'll fly out to Jenny's. Take her that present. Okay?"

A hint of a smile turned her lips, but she shook her head. "I can't let you do that. It's too expensive a gesture when none of this was your fault."

"But I want to do it. Come on, say yes."

Her smile blossomed, and excitement sparkled in her eyes. "Okay. You're on."

Yes. Getting Jenny's present to her as soon as possible wasn't much, but it was the one positive thing he could bring to this ugly mess. "Come on, let's get up this hill."

He helped Winnie up to the ridge's peak, praying there was someone at the cabin. For Winnie's sake. For Jenny's sake. And for his own sore conscience.

As the sun prepared to disappear for the night he peered anxiously down the slope, looking for the cabin.

He spotted it almost immediately. The small log

structure was tucked no more than a hundred feet down the slope. Unfortunately, no vehicle sat next to it. No sounds drifted from it. No lights shone from within. And even in the fading light he could see the shutters were pulled tight and locked against the marauding beasts, and possibly humans as well.

A soft cry slipped from Winnie's lips. "Oh, God, no one's home."

"Hey—" he placed a comforting hand on her shoulder "—let's not get disappointed yet. It might be that no one's home just now but will be back soon. Let's go see."

A steadying hand at Winnie's elbow, he headed down the slope, hoping, at the very least, the cabin was a weekend retreat and not a hunting cabin. If it was a weekend retreat, rescue might be just around the corner. But if it was a hunting cabin, used only a few times a year…

As soon as they hit the level ground of the meadow he let go of Winnie and jogged to the cabin. He leaped onto the porch and tried the latch on the rough-hewn wooden door. Locked.

Gritting his teeth in frustration, he strode to one of the small windows and tried to peer in. They were so dirty it was impossible to see through. He strode back to the door, stepped back…and kicked it in. It gave way with a loud crack and the sound of splintering wood.

Winnie gasped in surprise. But then she rushed to his side and they peered into the dark interior. A small round table with two chairs, a set of kitchen

cabinets, a small counter with a stainless steel sink
and a double bed huddled in the gloom.

A giant white sheet covered the bed, its hanging
edges touching the floor. Dust covered every sur-
face. The smell of must and rodent leavings rolled
over him like a giant wave.

It didn't look as if anyone had been here in years.
All hope of a timely rescue died.

"Damn." He sighed, leaning against the splin-
tered doorjamb. "I'm sorry."

She drew in a shaky breath, but when she looked
at him she had a brave smile plastered on her lips.
"Don't worry. It's not what we hoped for. But it is
a shelter. The bears won't eat us tonight." Her smile
got a little wider. "At least they won't once you
find a way to put the door back on."

He returned her smile, pleasure washing through
him at her sweet, resilient nature. Pleasure he had
no right to feel when in the end all he had to offer
her was…betrayal.

Chapter Five

Late the next morning Rand leaned against the rough bark of a proud pine and stared out at the clearing by the cabin and the grand Alaskan vista beyond. He'd been out here awhile. A long while. Being stuck inside the tiny enclosure with Winnie, watching her sleep, thinking how much he'd like to slip inside the tiny bed with her had been both temptation and torment. A special kind of hell that had made him crazy enough to howl at the moon. So he'd abandoned the cabin long before dawn.

The crisp morning air had goose bumps dancing over his skin, but he didn't mind. It was so beautiful here it was hard to mind something as benign as a little cold.

He was unhappy about this mission. And bloody unhappy Winnie had been hurt in the commission of it. But for once he had no complaints about the location he was stuck in. The bright morning sunshine glinted off the towering peaks of the snow-capped mountain range surrounding him and intensified the colors of the wild grasses and blooming wildflowers filling the small meadow next to the cabin.

He pulled in a deep breath of clean mountain air, his gaze settling on a clump of light blue flowers blooming near the center of the field. They were his favorite. The yellow and white flowers that covered most of the open field were bright and cheery, but the soft color of the blue flowers was comforting...peaceful.

Peace was a rare commodity in his life. When it happened along, he took the time to appreciate it.

Behind him the rusty hinges of the cabin door sounded. He turned his head to find Winnie stumbling out the door. "How do you feel?" Stupid question. She looked like hell. Her shoulders slumped in fatigue. Pain shadowed her eyes.

But she rallied to toss him a wry smile. "Like I crashed a plane into the bush yesterday. My head aches. My body aches. And my arm throbs with every beat of my heart. How about you?"

"I'm fine." He tipped his head toward her arm. "Any burning? We need to watch for infection."

She shook her head. "Just the aching I would expect, and you can't possibly be fine. No one is ever just fine after crashing a plane into the ground. There have to be bruises and aches and at the very least minor pains. So quit playing the macho man and tell me how you really feel.''

Guilt stung him. The last person she should be worrying about was him. He'd caused this whole damned mess. And the tiny injuries he'd gotten in the crash were nothing compared to hers...or the injuries he usually received in this job. *That,* of course, he couldn't tell her. So he forced a casual smile to his lips. ''I have a few bruises, and I'm a little stiff, thank you. You needn't worry about me, I'm fine. But you look like you're about to pass out. Why don't you sit down for a bit?''

''Good idea.'' She strode to the edge of the porch, sank down onto the top step and ran a shaky hand through her wild curls. ''This is ridiculous. I shouldn't feel this weak. After sleeping last night away—and half of the morning if the height of the sun means anything—I should be raring to go.''

''It's going to be a day or two before you're raring to go anywhere.''

''Well, it shouldn't be. I didn't even feel this bad yesterday after the crash.''

''You were running on adrenaline then. It's a hell of an anesthetic and energy booster, but it exacts its own toll. Your headache is typical of an adrenaline hangover. As for the rest, you can't expect to be anything but sore and tired after crashing the plane and hiking halfway across the state yesterday.''

"I suppose you're right, but still…it's frustrating."

"I know. Unfortunately, beyond the relief the aspirin in the first-aid kit can offer, I can't do much to help the pain in your arm. But caffeine will help the fatigue and headache." He nodded his head toward the campfire he'd started early this morning. "There was coffee in your survival pack. You up for some?"

"Not until I manage to stumble out to the outhouse. And I don't have the energy to stand up yet."

He smiled. "I can help you out there, if you're in dire straits."

She shook her head, an embarrassed smile turning her lips. "If the time comes when I can't get to the outhouse by myself, just shoot me, will ya?"

He chuckled and dropped down beside her on the step. "I don't think it will come to anything so drastic."

They sat companionably on the steps, listening to the birds chirp overhead and watching two squirrels fight over a goodie they'd found beneath a pile of leaves.

Her heat soaked into his shoulder, chasing his goose bumps and the lingering morning chill away. He leaned a little closer, not enough that she'd notice or feel crowded, but close enough to catch more of her heat. He drank in that warmth and the clean mountain air and the gentle sway of the blue flowers as the birds chirped overhead.

It was an idyllic moment. One that tempted him

to put the mission on hold. Pretend he was just a man who'd crashed in the woods with a beautiful woman for a few days. A man whose biggest dilemma was whether or not he should follow his instincts and kiss the woman. He smiled. It was an instinct he'd very much like to follow. Her innocence and sweetness were tempting lures. Ones that were a little harder to resist with each passing hour.

She gently bumped his shoulder with her own. "I'm sorry about this mess and whatever crimp it's put in your plans. Hopefully, we won't be here long. I filed a flight plan for the charter, so half an hour after I didn't check in from your lodge, they would have had planes out looking for us. I'm sure someone will find us soon." She looked at the sky, worry pulling her brow low.

He didn't mind that rescue hadn't arrived. Wouldn't mind if it didn't arrive before the blue flowers quit blooming and all their petals fell away and drifted to the ground. But he didn't want Winnie worrying. "They'll get here. And until they do we have everything we need. Food, water, shelter. We'll be fine."

"I suppose, but I hate the thought of causing everyone so much grief. Henry's probably beside himself." She groaned softly. "His poor plane. And what about you? Were you supposed to check in with anyone yesterday once you got to the lodge? Will people be concerned about you? Fretting that you're hurt?"

Fatigue stole through him. The idyllic moment

was over. She'd just opened the perfect door for him to get to work. He looked away from the blue flowers and settled his gaze on the shadows beneath the pines as his mind automatically pieced together an answer from the cover story they'd come up with for this mission. "You needn't worry about that. I'm here on vacation. I thought two weeks of being away from it all would be nice. No one expects to hear from me until I get back."

The lies rolled so easily off his tongue. "What about you? Is someone sitting by a phone waiting for the rescue workers to call and say you're found, hail and hearty? Mom? Dad?"

She shook her head. "My mom passed away five years ago. And my father and I are estranged."

He lifted a brow. "That doesn't sound good."

She shrugged. "Actually, it is good."

He shot her a questioning look, hoping she'd explain. He knew, of course, that she and her father were estranged. It was in the file the CIA had on her. But he didn't know *why* they were estranged. And the more he knew about her, the easier it would be for him to steer her in the direction he needed.

She stared at the forest, anger pulling the corners of her lips down, sadness shadowing her eyes. "Let's just say that if my dad shows up on your doorstep, the smartest thing to do is zip your billfold and run the other way."

"Your frown makes me think that's more than a casual observation."

"Hard-learned life lesson, I'm afraid."

"Learned early in life or more recently?"

She laughed humorlessly. "Well, you'd think I would have figured it out earlier. I certainly watched my father come home for a few weeks and then leave with whatever savings my mother had managed to scrape together often enough to have figured out his game. But you know, hope springs eternal. And children want to believe their daddies love them."

"And you're sure yours didn't?"

"I think it's a pretty safe bet to say the only person my father has ever loved is himself." She shook her head. "For years I thought if I behaved well enough, got good enough grades at school, was nice enough to him when he came home, he'd actually stay. But he never did. He only came home when he needed money. And he didn't stay any longer than it took for him to reassert his charm with my mother. Then he was gone, right along with the money. But sadly, that wasn't enough to convince me the man was best avoided."

His heart ached at the thought of Winnie as a little girl trying so hard to earn her father's love. Trying again and again only to fail. The last thing he wanted to do was drag her down that path again. But working undercover was about collecting information, as much information as the agent could dig up, so he pressed on. "What finally convinced you?"

She waved away the question. "It's a long story."

He gave her a wry smile. "We're not going anywhere."

She chuckled softly. "No, I guess we aren't. Okay, let's see, where to start. Like I said, it didn't occur to me when I was younger that I wasn't the cause of my father's long absences. So as I got older I thought of different ways to try to keep him around. When I was sixteen I learned to fly, thinking if we just had something in common, some bond we shared, he'd at least stay a little longer during his visits."

"I take it your dad was a pilot?" Rand knew, of course, that her father was an aerobatics pilot. But Bob Smith didn't know that.

She nodded. "My dad had a Chipmunk, a cute little aerobatics plane. He made his living performing at air shows."

"Sounds like fun. Did becoming a pilot work? Did he stay home more?"

She shook her head. "Nah. He did spend a little more time with me, though, talking about the sport. To me that was a huge improvement if not a complete success. Which just made me immerse myself in flying more. Even started doing aerobatics once I could afford it. Which eventually led to my father asking me to join him on the circuit."

"Did you?" She had and he knew it. The fact that The Racing Bullets had taken the air show circuit by storm the first year they'd started performing was in the CIA file. So was the fact that the team had broken up just two years after their inception.

But there was no explanation for the team's breakup in the report. *That* was the information he was digging for.

"Are you kidding? Father and daughter together at last? Fool that I was I jumped at the chance."

"I take it there was a catch."

"There always is with my dad. And it's always the same. Money and a free ride—for him. As a kid growing up it never occurred to me that the reason my father could spend so much time traveling all over the country was because he didn't have a job. Nor did it occur to me that the reason he never had any money, and therefore had to steal it from my mother, was because he didn't have a job. In other words, I was blind to the fact that my father was basically a lazy, shiftless man. A lazy, shiftless man who used his charm to get others to support him in life.

"But that fact was impossible to ignore when we were working together. He'd disappear for days, sometimes weeks at a time, leaving me to deal with the show coordinators and the millions of details that go into getting ready to fly a show. And he'd miss practice sessions all the time, showing up at the show expecting us to fly stunts we'd never done in the air together before. It was exhausting trying to keep everything together all by myself. The only thing I could count on him doing was picking up our paycheck. He was always there for that. But was he ever around at the beginning of the month, when the bills were due? No-o-o."

She grimaced in self-disgust. "I can't tell you how many times I had to get an extra job so I could cover the bills. So the bank wouldn't come repossess our planes. Sheesh. I should have let them take them."

"So what happened to break up the team?"

"The usual. Dad spied a greener pasture and split, leaving me holding a fistful of mechanic and fuel bills along with the bank notes on two aerobatic planes. *That's* when I finally figured out avoiding my father was the best thing for both my mental and financial health. I haven't spoken to him since. And I don't plan to anytime soon."

A sad but sound decision from what he'd heard. "So Daddy's thankfully out of the picture. But what about the air shows? Are you still flying them? Or did you have to sell the planes?" Another fact he knew but Bob Smith didn't.

"Giving the planes to the bank and walking away would have been the easiest answer to the debt. But I didn't want to give up aerobatics. I love flying the air shows. So I gave one of the planes to the bank, changed the name on the other one, went solo and worked my tail off to pay it off."

"But you don't do air shows full-time?"

"It's actually pretty hard to earn a living that way. And it's a grueling existence. Plus, a man came along and I got married. His job demanded he travel a lot, so I thought it would be best if I worked close to home. That way I could be home when he was."

She laughed, a cold, humorless sound. "For all the good that did me."

"Ouch. Doesn't sound like that turned out any better than the partnership with your dad did." It was a smooth, easy transition to the subject he most needed to probe, and he was going to take full advantage of it.

He was convinced she hadn't been involved in dear ol' Tuck's heist, but he didn't know how Tucker had left her life. Didn't know if she'd seen him after the sting or if he'd just disappeared from her world. She might well have clues to his whereabouts. And if she did, he needed them.

She shrugged. "Actually, I guess it was pretty similar. Like Daddy, Tucker left for greener pastures. Except the lure in his pasture wasn't more green, it was a pretty little filly."

Adrenaline snaked through him. Another woman? That was an important detail. "Someone you knew?"

She shook her head. "No, thank God. I never saw her, and he never mentioned her name. He just showed up a few months ago, told me he'd found someone else, packed his bags and left."

He needed to zero in on the leaving part. See if Tucker had dropped any hints about where he and his new sweetheart were going. But before he could pose his next question she pushed up from the porch. "I think I can manage the rest of that walk now." She headed down the small path that led to the outhouse behind the cabin.

Damn, just when things were going so well. "I'll pour the coffee while you're gone." Maybe he could coax a few more details out of her while she drank the hot brew and got rid of her headache.

"Thanks." She stopped and turned back to him, an easy smile turning her lips. "I want to thank you for cleaning the cabin up last night and getting clean linens on the bed so I could sleep. I was done in by the time I got here, and I can't tell you how much I appreciate not having to sleep on mouse droppings."

He waved her thanks away. It was the last thing he deserved. "It was nothing."

She shook her head. "It was something. I saw how hard you worked. And I appreciate it." She flashed him an easy grin. "You're a veritable prince."

Yeah, a veritable prince. He'd put her through hell and was manipulating her with every word out of his mouth. Which just made the fact that he wanted to pull her into his arms and comfort her that much worse. Comfort her? Hell, he wanted to kiss her. Kiss her until she forgot the sadness her father had caused, forgot the hurt her ex had inflicted. Kiss her until he forgot the loneliness in his own heart.

God, he was worse than her old man and dear ol' Tuck put together.

Chapter Six

The next afternoon Winnie trimmed the stems of the wildflowers she'd picked earlier. No rescue plane had flown overhead yesterday and none this morning, either. She hadn't even heard the drone of a distant engine.

Not good. Henry must be worried to death, wondering what had happened to them. And his plane. She winced, thinking of the burning frame they'd left behind and wished someone would find them soon. There would be a million consequences from the crash, none of them good. She'd just as soon get them behind her.

Shaking off those dark thoughts, she stuck the small bouquet into a glass of water in the middle of the table. There. The table was set. And all and all, it looked pretty good.

The small cache of blue enamelware plates and cups the owner of the cabin kept wasn't fancy, but the bright blue specks of enamel and the blue flowers she'd taken from the field made a pretty setting in their own rustic way.

She smiled as she moved to the stove where lunch bubbled in a small cast-iron pot. She'd raided the cupboards for the plates and picked the flowers because she wanted to do something nice for Smith.

Despite the caffeine she'd poured into her system yesterday, she'd slept most of the day away, while he'd kept the campfire going and fixed their meals and patrolled the camp for bears.

Chuckling to herself, she grabbed a pot holder and lifted the hot pot from the stove. He'd made it clear he thought the "bear patrol" was a complete waste of time, but he'd taken his rifle and dutifully done it anyway. Because he knew it made her feel better. Fixing him a nice lunch was the least she could do.

She grimaced at the reconstituted stew in the pot. The packets of freeze-dried food in the survival gear—of which this meal was part—definitely did not qualify as nice, but it was the best she could manage out here. Still carrying the pot, she strode to the cabin door and leaned out.

Smith was sitting on the porch steps, staring out at the field.

She hadn't been conscious a lot yesterday, but the few times she had been she'd found him thus. Sitting here on the porch or leaning against a big pine, staring out at the countryside. She couldn't see his face now, but she'd seen his expression enough yesterday to know what was there. A deep, abiding appreciation. And something else she couldn't quite name. Longing perhaps.

But whatever held him enthralled she would have to disturb it. Lunch was going to be bad enough hot, cold it would be inedible. "Lunch is ready."

He turned to look at her, his gaze sweeping her from head to foot, looking for signs that she'd overtaxed herself.

She rolled her eyes and shook her head. "Stop it. I told you I'm fine."

A smile turned his lips. "So you did. I just didn't want you pushing yourself if you didn't feel up to it. I could have fixed lunch."

"I know. You fixed all the meals yesterday and this morning, remember? And did it well, I might add. But now it's my turn."

"Good enough."

She tried desperately not to notice the breadth of his shoulders or the enticing play of hard muscles as he pushed to his feet. Or the powerful, fluid way he moved as he made his way to the door. And the feminine shivers his heat created as he passed her at the door—she was definitely ignoring that.

Of course, it would be a whole lot easier to ignore those things if the man wasn't so nice. But he was nice. Really nice. And ignoring him was getting harder. Not the best of circumstances for someone trying to build an independent life.

She took a protective step back and drew a deep breath to regain her senses as he strode toward the table with that panther grace. Halfway there, he came to a sudden halt.

When he didn't move on, she strode around him and peeked at his face.

He was staring at the table, surprise lighting his features. "I was expecting the usual meal in a pouch. But this is very nice. Real plates. Flowers even." He turned to her with a warm smile. "You went all out."

She smiled back, feeling much more pleased than she should at his simple pleasure. She waved an anxious hand toward the table. "I couldn't help but notice you seemed pretty impressed with those flowers. You were so careful to make sure they ended up in the middle of the *O* in the SOS we trampled into the field for the rescue planes this morning and *not* in the path of the weeds we tromped down. I thought you might like a few on the table."

"I do. They're the perfect touch in this humble abode." He strode to the table and dropped into one of the chairs.

She ladled stew onto their plates and set the pot back on the small wood-burning stove. "I thought so, too. But then I love wildflowers. The way they pop up out of nowhere and there they are—a little spot of color. This spring when I moved into the cabin I'm renting I bought a can of wildflower seeds and tossed them in my front yard. I was amazed to see how many of them actually came up. And two weeks ago some of them started blooming. It's great fun seeing what opens up from day to day.''

"Sounds pretty.''

"It is.'' She took a bite of the stew, trying not to notice how perfectly tasteless it was, hoping the setting would make up for the less-than-fantastic fare.

Smith forked a giant bite of the stew into his mouth with what looked like real enthusiasm.

Enthusiasm she was sure would die as soon as he really tasted what he was eating. They hadn't tried the stew before, but it was the same as the meals they'd fixed yesterday. Hard in some places, mushy in others, absolutely, positively tasteless. Yuk.

But Smith forked up a second bite with the same enthusiasm as the last, chewed a couple of times and swallowed with what looked like genuine relish.

She stared at him as if he was a rather odd, curious animal at the zoo. Finally she said, "You must be a bachelor.''

He looked up from his plate. "Why's that?''

"Because you're eating that food as if it has some value other than straight, unadorned nutrition.''

"It's good.''

Her eyes popped wide. "You're kidding, right?''

He shook his head. "No. It's good. And even if it wasn't—which is not the case—I'd still eat it like it was ambrosia. You went to a lot of trouble—cooking it on the stove, picking the flowers, setting the table—I'd never insult you by being anything less than enthusiastic.''

She stared at him, warm, feminine tingles shivering through her. The kind of tingles that made her want to smile and giggle and forget the harsh realities of the real world. The kind of tingles that got a girl in trouble when a man like Smith was near. She scowled in frustration. ''I wish you wouldn't do that.''

''What?''

''Be so nice about everything.''

''What's so nice about simple courtesy? Someone goes out of their way for you, you appreciate it.''

She laughed, sadly, bitterly. ''Trust me, not everyone bothers.''

''Do I hear a bit of the big bad ex in that lament?''

She smiled wryly. If anything was guaranteed to keep those incorrigible little tingles in control it was talking about Tucker. ''Yeah, you do. I can't tell you how many times I spent an entire day fixing a special meal for him, and the rat wouldn't even notice. Or he'd say something like, tomorrow night, why don't you fix a steak, like what he was eating, what I'd spent hours preparing, was a burger I'd picked up at Mickey D's or something.''

He shrugged those big, sexy shoulders. ''If he was so unappreciative, why did you keep doing it? Why not just pick something up at Mickey D's for him?''

Yeah, why hadn't she? She shook her head. ''I don't know. I guess I never could convince myself that at some level he didn't appreciate it. Plus, I wanted things to be nice for him when he came home.''

"That's right, you mentioned he traveled. What did he do?''

She took another bite of the dismal stew. "He worked for the CIA.''

He cocked a brow. "Really? That's interesting.''

She tipped a shoulder. "It would have been if he'd ever told me what he did when he was in the field. But he didn't. Said it was all top secret. He never shared any of it.''

He shot her a hopeful look. "You sure? A few good spy stories could help while away the hours here.''

She laughed at his boyish enthusiasm. What was it about men and spy stories? "Sorry, can't help you. Tucker kept *everything* to himself. Where he was going, what he was working on, when he'd be home. Everything.'' A hint of the bitterness she'd always felt at being kept out of such a huge part of Tucker's life crept into her voice.

Concern pulled his brows low. "Hey, it probably was top secret. And it probably was best you didn't know.''

She shrugged. "That's what I thought at the time. But I don't believe it anymore. While I'm sure there was top secret information he couldn't share, I can't possibly imagine there was anything top secret about when he was coming home.

"Considering the way he left, I think he kept me

in the dark so he could move around at will. After all, if I didn't know when his mission was over, it would be easy for him to grab some time for himself. Time he eventually used to plan a new life." She tried to keep the sadness from her words, but it was there nonetheless.

He studied her from across the table, his gaze intense. "Maybe. But if you ask me, the saddest thing about your husband's leaving is that he didn't do it years before. The guy sounds like a jerk. He didn't share his life with you. Didn't notice when you went out of the way for him. Ran off with another woman. You're well rid of him."

She undoubtedly was. But she'd loved Tucker Taylor. She'd looked forward to his retirement and the time they would finally have together. The death of that dream had left a hole in her heart. A big hole that ached and reminded her, once again, that whatever it took to keep a man's love, she didn't have it.

She pushed that melancholy thought away. Tucker was gone. She'd given him four years of her life. That was enough. Especially when there was such an intriguing man sitting across the table from her. "So, Mr. Smith, enough of my boring domestic life. It's your turn to talk now. Tell me about yourself."

"Not much to tell."

"Ah, a modest man. Commendable." She shot him a teasing smile. "But not very useful for table conversation. Tell me what you do for a living."

He hesitated, just for a second, and the corners of his mouth seemed to tip down. But then she blinked and the faint scowl was gone. With another shrug he said, "I'm a freelance photojournalist."

"Wow. That's interesting. What was your last job? Catching the latest 'deep throat' at work? Documenting the lives of the rich and famous?"

His smile turned wry. "Nothing so exciting or glamorous."

"No? What then?"

The corners of his lips dipped down again, more pronounced this time. "Shooting the flora and fauna of the Colombian jungle. Neither glamorous nor exciting."

She cocked her head, studying him. "Okay, not glamorous or exciting maybe, but it certainly sounds interesting. Exotic. Lush jungles, blooming orchids, half-naked tribesmen. What's not to love?"

He shook his head. "Plenty, I assure you. While they look great on film those lush jungles are hot and humid and filled with biting, stinging insects and rotting vegetation. As for the half-naked tribesmen, many of them are toting machine guns and looking for someone to use as target practice."

She'd forgotten Colombia's economy was fueled by illegal drug money. And that the political climate was anything but peaceful and serene. Corrupt government officials, leftist rebels and right-wing thugs all fighting for power and backing up their interests with violence and heavy firearms. She wrinkled her nose. "Not much fun, huh?"

He shook his head. "Not much fun."

"We'll move on to something more pleasant then. Where do you live?"

"Here and there mostly. You never know when or where that prize-winning photo is going to pop up. Now, can we possibly talk about something more interesting than me?"

She couldn't think of anything more interesting than him. Which was probably the best reason to move on to a new topic. She grabbed hold of the first thing that came to mind. A rather worrisome topic. "So, do you think our rescue signals will work?"

He nodded, his expression reassuring. "Positive. The smoke fire we built next to our SOS should attract attention. If one of the rescue planes flies over, they'll know they've found us."

"What if no one flies over?" She couldn't help but voice her worst fear.

He looked up from his plate, locking his gaze confidently on hers. "Winnie, they're going to find us."

She shook her head at her uncharacteristic paranoia. "You're right, they are. But could they do it already? I'd like Henry to know we're okay. He's the one person who *will* be worrying about us." She grimaced, thinking Henry was going to get as much bad news as good when they got back.

Smith reached across the table and laid his hand over hers, giving it a gentle squeeze. "You worrying about Henry's reaction to losing his plane?"

She nodded, letting his heat and strength soak into her.

"Well, don't. Henry seems like a reasonable man. He's going to understand you did the best you could with the plane on fire and no decent place to land. I'll damned well make sure he knows you saved our lives."

Tears stung her eyes. With a father who'd never been around, a mother who'd been so devastated by her husband's abandonment that she'd barely functioned and a husband who'd always been out saving the world, she'd pretty much faced life and its difficulties by herself. But Smith made her feel as if she had an ally in the world. A friend. It was a novel feeling. A good feeling. She squeezed his hand in return. "Thanks, I'd appreciate that."

"No problem. Now, I'll tell you what, I want to spend the afternoon collecting wood in case rescue doesn't come immediately. We need it for cooking, and I want to leave as much wood in the owner's woodpile as was here when we arrived. Maybe a little more. But if we're still here tomorrow morning, I think we should do something fun. I found a little stream yesterday while I was out on bear patrol. It wanders through the woods about half a mile down the hill on the other side of the field." Mischief sparkled in his eyes, making him look like a ten-year-old proposing a day of hooky. "Let's go fishing."

Fishing? Sharp hooks, smelly bait and slimy fish? She should be appalled at the thought. But fishing with Bob Smith? Those giddy little tingles raced through her.

Which is why she should say no. No, no, *no.*

But she didn't want to say no. Not with his heat soaking into her where their hands joined. Not with the promise of fun and adventure sparkling in his eyes. She gave his hand another squeeze. "Yeah, fishing sounds like fun."

Chapter Seven

The next morning Rand strode through the forest down the narrow deer path with Winnie trailing behind him. He was carrying the rifle—making sure those bears didn't get them—while Winnie carried the short, telescoping rod that had been in the survival gear and the small tackle box with its selection of bait and lures.

Fishing.

He loved the sport. And he was excited about sharing it with Winnie. But he was a little apprehensive, too. He didn't want to railroad her into something she didn't want to do. He'd already put her through enough misery. He glanced over his shoulder. "Are you sure you want to do this?"

"Do what? Go fishing? Of course I do."

Maybe she did. But the truth was he knew damned few women who did. And he didn't want her pretending she liked the sport just to make him happy. And he feared she would.

While he'd learned little about Tucker Taylor since this whole fiasco began—despite his efforts to get Winnie to talk about her past—he'd learned a lot about the woman next to him. She was pretty, sexy and...she wanted to make those around her happy. She'd spent years cooking fancy meals for a man who didn't appreciate it, carried boxes across miles of wilderness with an injured arm for a motherless child and went out of her way to fix a nice lunch for a man who was lying to her at every turn. Not that she knew he was lying, but still... "I'm just saying if you don't want to do this, we don't have to."

She chuckled softly. "Listen, this is your vacation time. You're supposed to be spending it at Markham's Lodge relaxing, having the time of your life. Which I'm guessing, since the place is renowned for its blue-ribbon trout streams, probably meant dipping a pole or two, right?"

Guilt slid through him. Going to Markham's Lodge had only been a ploy to have her fly him somewhere. He'd brought his rod, yes. He would have fished, absolutely. But no matter how good the fishing was, after twenty-four hours he would have called Henry's charter service and asked to be flown somewhere else. And that little plan had gotten them stranded here.

Which is why he didn't want her putting herself through another ordeal for him. "I'll tell you what. You give it a chance, and if you still hate it after an hour, we'll call it quits."

She rolled her eyes. "I'll tell *you* what, I hate it in an hour, *I'll* call it quits. You keep fishing, I'll find my way back to the cabin."

He raised a surprised brow and held up the rifle she'd made sure he had before they left the cabin. "What about the bears?"

She drew in a sharp hiss. "Good point. Change of plan. If I hate it I'll lounge back on the bank and spend the afternoon watching *you* fish."

He shot her a wry look. "Now doesn't that sound like fun?"

A smile lit her features, and she chuckled softly. "Trust me, if I get to help eat the catch, it won't be that big a hardship."

A smile tugged at his lips. She did seem to hate the freeze-dried food packed in the survival gear. She might well think an afternoon of sitting on the bank was worth her time. "Okay, deal." He stuck out his hand.

She shook it with enthusiasm.

The heat from her hand warmed his palm almost as much as her smile touched something else deep inside him. And the softness of her skin... He quickly released her hand. He didn't need a reminder of just how long it had been since he'd been with a woman. Particularly a woman as beautiful and sweet and innocent as Winnie.

She nodded toward the arm he dropped to his side. "You've got goose bumps again. The Alaskan climate is a little chilly for you."

He shrugged. "It's a big change from the Colombian jungle." The advantage to using the photojournalist cover was that he wouldn't have to hide where he'd been. Or construct an entire past. A photojournalist could easily have been in many places he'd been in, seen many of the events he'd been involved in.

"I can see how the change in temperature would be a shock to your system. You should have grabbed one of the blankets from the survival gear and worn it like a serape. It would have kept you warm."

He shook his head. "I don't mind the chill. It's a good reminder that I'm *not* in the jungle anymore. And it'll warm up soon."

They were close enough to the stream that they could hear its cheery gurgle echoing through the forest. Anticipation ran through his veins. He preferred fly fishing. A quiet stream, a well-tied fly and hours of watching his line arc through the air. But he'd take the sport any way it came. "Come on. The stream's right through here." He headed off the path, made his way down a small incline and then pushed his way through a few small bushes, pulling Winnie behind him. "This is it."

Winnie looked around at the wide, grassy bank

and the meandering stream a mere ten feet in front of them. "Pretty."

Yes, it was. In fact the whole scene was idyllic. A secluded, pine-scented forest. A bubbling brook. A beautiful woman. And a fishing rod. Life didn't get better than this.

He leaned the rifle against a nearby pine and took the rod from Winnie. "Okay, let's get this show on the road." He was anxious to share the sport with her. Hoped she would enjoy it just a tenth as much as he.

Pulling the hook from where it was stuck securely into the cork handle, he released the lock on the reel, stripped out some line and began telescoping the rod out to its full length. He shook his head as he pulled the last section of blue graphite tight, making sure the thing wouldn't collapse during casting. "This is the most ridiculous rod I've ever seen."

"Hey, don't complain. We could be tying string to the end of a long stick and using God-knows-what for a hook."

He laughed softly. "You're right. And while this rod does nothing for my sense of sportsmanship, I have to say I'm duly impressed with the survival kit the FAA makes you carry. Blankets, food, water, a tent and just about every tool imaginable for procuring food. Rifle, fishing pole, fishing net even. Amazingly thorough for a government agency."

She smiled. "Isn't it, though? But as Henry explained to me—and as we've so unfortunately discovered—planes go down in Alaska all the time.

And sometimes it takes weeks for rescue to arrive. The FAA doesn't want people starving to death before the cavalry arrives.''

"And aren't we glad?'' He grabbed the hook. "Okay, let's get some bait on this thing.''

She wrinkled her nose. "We're not talking worms here, are we?''

He shook his head. "What do women have against worms?''

"You mean besides the fact they're slimy, dirty and disgusting?''

He chuckled. "Fish think they're juicy, well seasoned and delicious. But, lucky you, we're going to use a cleaner type of bait today.'' He nodded toward the case she was still carrying. "There's a jar of fish roe in there. Let's start with that.''

"Fish roe, huh?'' She grabbed a jar from the small tackle box. "This?''

"Yep.''

She held the jar in front of her, studying the bright-red fish eggs. "Pretty.''

He smiled at the assessment. "We might make a fisherman out of you, yet.'' He quickly baited the hook and moved to the river's edge. "Come on, I'll show you how to cast and then I'm going to hand the rod over to you.''

She stepped up beside him, her expression a bit wary, but there was interest there, too.

Yes. He held the rod in front of him, demonstrating the correct hold, his shoulder bumping hers. "Okay, casting is pretty simple. I'm sure you've seen it done. The important thing to remember is to hit the release lever here on the reel as you cast forward.'' He pointed to the long lever directly under his thumb. ''That releases your line so it can strip out of the reel and your hook can end up somewhere in the river instead of at your feet. Got it?''

She nodded, her expression intent.

''Okay, watch.'' He drew the pole back over his shoulder then cast forward, hitting the release. The high pitch of stripping line sang in his ears. He smiled, relishing the simple act. Relishing the fresh air and warm sun and excellent company.

The baited hook sailed freely through the air and landed just a few inches from the far bank. Perfect. ''Now, as soon as the bait's in the water, you turn this little crank here.'' He turned the small crank on the side of the reel until it locked. ''Hear that click?''

''Yep.''

''That's the reel locking, which keeps your line from continuing to strip out and ending up halfway down the stream in a tangled mess. As soon as your bait's in the water, you lock it in place. Got it?''

''Yep.''

''Now, when you're bait fishing in a stream, you cast downstream and as near to the far bank as possible.''

''What's wrong with the middle of the stream? Providing I can even get the thing that far.''

He smiled at her beginner's lack of confidence. ''Don't worry, you're going to do just fine. As for why, watch the line.'' He pointed to where the line disappeared into the water very near the middle of the stream now. ''See how the current is carrying it back toward us? Soon it will have made its way all the way back to our bank. At that point you reel it in so it doesn't sink to the bottom and get caught on a log or rock or whatever. Got it?''

She nodded, her gaze locked on the rod as if it might hold a few dangers he hadn't mentioned.

He smiled encouragingly. ''Relax, fishing is fun, not rocket science. There's no such thing as a big mistake here.'' The line neared their bank. He reeled it in and held the rod out to her. ''Your turn.''

She wiped her hands on her jeans and then took the rod. ''Why don't you go stand down there?'' She pointed to a spot a bit downstream.

''Relax, I'm fine here.'' He didn't want to go down there. He wanted to stand here. By her. Soak in her heat, her apprehensive excitement.

She shook her head. ''I'll feel better if you go down there. I'm afraid I'll hook you. And while that might not be a big mistake on a cosmic scale, I'll bet it would be a painful one.''

With a light chuckle he reluctantly moved down the bank. Not because he was afraid she would hook him, but because it would make her feel better, give her the confidence to really cast the line. ''Okay, fire away.''

Her face was a study in concentration as she adjusted her footing, carefully angled the rod back, hesitated and then cast forward. She hit the release a little late, but still the baited hook made it to the middle of the stream where it hit the water with a soft plop.

She turned to him with an excited shimmy and a smile so brilliant he would have thought she'd cast halfway across one of the Great Lakes. "I did it."

"You sure did." He recognized her smile. He'd worn it himself when he'd first learned the sport. Warmth slid through him. His father and grandfather had taught him how to fish. They'd shared old fish tales and secret techniques as they'd stood hip deep in rushing water or sat before campfires eating the day's catch. Those had been some of the best days of his life.

After his disastrous stab at civilian life, after he'd realized there would never be a family for him, he'd wondered if he would ever share the sport with anyone again. But he was sharing it now. He'd have this day to add to those memories. He tipped his head toward the rod. "Don't forget to set the reel. Turn the crank until it clicks."

She turned the crank a half turn, hesitated and then started cranking it in earnest.

"Just until it clicks," he reminded.

She shook her head. "I'm going to reel it in and recast."

Ahhh, the joys of learning to cast. He remembered them well. "Okay, have at it."

This time she hit the release earlier and the bait went farther. Not much farther. Nowhere near the far bank yet, but past the middle. She turned to him with an even wider smile. "Better!"

His mind flashed back to his childhood. He was little, seven maybe, and it was his first fishing trip. His dad was standing on the bank next to him while he practiced casting. Every time the baited hook had gone another inch he'd felt like a conquering hero. And his father—the man who had outcast him every day of his life—had smiled and patted him on the back and made him think his minor progress was nothing short of wondrous. He'd forgotten how good such innocent wonder felt. Until this moment.

He shot Winnie a thumbs-up and a brilliant smile of his own. "Good job. Now don't forget to set your reel."

She did and then let the bait sit for about ten seconds before she started reeling it in again. The next cast went a little farther still, and she turned to him with an accusatory glare. "So what is your beef with this pole? It's a wonderful pole. Perfect in fact."

An arrow in his heart. He shot her a look of mock horror. "Blasphemy, woman. That thing you're holding is a cheap imitation of the real thing. And it's called a fishing *rod,* not a pole."

She rolled her eyes. "Oh please, rod, pole, what difference does it make as long as it has wire, reel and hook?"

He winced. "Line. Fishing *line.* And it matters. A true fisherman chooses his rod as carefully as he chooses his woman. It has to look right and have the right feel and respond just so when he holds it in his hands. That thing you're holding fills no more than the most basic requirements. It's like a quickie in a back alley. It takes off the edge, but has no aesthetics or romance or heart or soul. In short, it's good in a pinch but no man would want to live with the thing.''

Her eyes popped wide and then she dissolved into throaty laughter, the sound echoing through the forest. "I am not going to touch that remark with a ten-foot pole. Or rod, either."

He shook his head, laughing. "What can I say, a man's rod and the women in his life sooner or later end up on the same page. At least we hope they do."

She shook her head, still chuckling. "Okay, enough, already. Tell me how I'll know if I get a fish."

He shook his head, smiling. "You're never going to catch anything if you don't stop casting every five seconds. The bait has to actually stay in the water long enough for a fish to see it for him to hit on it."

Her brows crashed together in disappointment. "But casting's all the fun."

She'd love fly fishing. It was all about casting. If his rod hadn't gone up with the plane he could have shown her, but... "Well, have fun, then. And you might get lucky, a fish might swim past with his mouth open just as you toss your bait in. You might snag one that way."

"Ah, the Zen way of fishing. I like it." She reeled

in with added gusto and a smile that stretched from one ear to the other.

He laughed, watching her cast with damned little finesse but bursting enthusiasm. He should be pulling information out of her. She was so preoccupied with the new thrill of fishing it would be easy. She'd answer whatever questions he threw her way without even realizing what she was saying.

His gut clenched. He didn't want to taint this moment with betrayal. He didn't want to taint this moment by bringing the job into it at all.

And he wasn't going to.

Not now. And not later, either, dammit. Not until someone came and found them. There would be plenty of time after the rescue to betray her. He couldn't do it here. Not in this pristine setting. Not with her smiling at him like that. She was having too much fun.

And so was he.

He wanted to stride across the distance between them, pull her into his arms and make love to her in the soft grass with the sun shining down on their naked bodies. At the very least he wanted to pull her into his arms and kiss her. Feel the softness of her body against him, taste her sweetness.

He wouldn't do it, of course. Stealing an innocent moment of bliss was one thing. Stealing a kiss... something else altogether. But he was going to steal this time for himself.

Not the wisest decision. This job had a habit of biting agents on the butt who broke the rules. And getting involved with the target was definitely breaking the rules. But right now, right this minute, with the sun on his face and Winnie having the time of her life, he didn't give a damn. He needed this, needed to feel like a normal human being, if only for a week or a day or a minute.

Chapter Eight

The next afternoon Winnie sat on the porch next to Smith as they ate their lunch. The sun was high in the sky. The air warm. Her spirits high—despite the fact rescue had not yet come their way. A little fact that, at the moment, didn't bother her a bit. She was having the time of her life. And she was having it...*fishing!* Who'da thought.

Of course, the man who'd been fishing with her, the man sitting next to her now, had had a lot to do with how much fun she'd had. He'd been generous and funny and unbelievably patient as he'd stood on the bank watching her cast again and again and *again*.

She smiled. He'd teased her about not being able

to catch a fish that way, but this morning when they'd wandered down to the stream again, she'd made him eat those words. It might, of course, have happened just the way he'd said, that a fish had been swimming by with its mouth open when she dropped the bait in the water, because the giant tug on her rod had come just seconds after she'd cast, but she didn't care *how* she'd caught it, only that she had.

She'd had as much fun reeling that giant fish in as she'd had the first time she'd pushed her stunt plane through a Lumcevak. Maybe more fun. Because she'd been alone in the air that day.

Her father was supposed to have come and helped talk her through the tricky maneuver. But, as usual, he hadn't shown up. Some sweet thing had snagged his attention before he'd made it to the airfield. So Winnie had taken her plane up and learned the stunt by herself. It had been exhilarating as the plane had tumbled through the air. The victory had been sweet—but it had been solitary.

This morning Smith had been at the river with her, his smile every bit as wide as her own. She remembered the wiggly weight of the fish as she'd pulled him from the stream and tried not to smile like a fool as she took another bite of her lunch. Not fresh trout, but freeze-dried ham and beans out of the pouch. The survival fare didn't taste any better today, but she didn't mind eating it as much.

She nudged Smith's shoulder gently with her

own. "You're not mad at me are you, for letting the fish go?"

A crooked smile turned his lips. "I'm not the one who minds eating this stuff. I let fish go all the time. In fact, I let them go far more than I keep them."

"Really?" Somehow she hadn't pictured Smith as a man who let his catch go. Perhaps it was his air of danger, the sense that he'd been in tight spots and walked away intact that made her think he was one of those men who, by God, ate their catch. Or hung it on the wall.

But he only shrugged at her surprise. "Really. Fishing isn't about trophies. Not to me, anyway. It's about breathtaking sunrises and rushing water and shared comradery. Old skills and old traditions and getting away from a world that is too fast and too crowded and sometimes too damned brutal."

She stared at him. "Wow. I think I was too excited to get all that."

He chuckled. "Don't worry. You keep at it, you'll get it."

She might. But right now she wanted to hear more about his experiences. And she knew just where she wanted to start. "So, Mr. Zen fisherman, tell me about your precious fishing rod. Any man who compares a fishing rod to a woman as *quaintly* if not eloquently as you did yesterday must have a special one of his own."

A shadow crossed his features, and his fork halted halfway to his mouth. But then he blinked, and when he lifted his gaze to hers there was nothing but a teasing sparkle there. "I'm not sure I should share anything quite so personal with you."

She rolled her eyes and bumped his knee with her own. "Quit being such a brat and tell me. I want to hear."

"Okay, but if you get bored I don't want to hear it. It would be too much for my ego to think a woman wasn't as enamored of my rod as I am."

She laughed and bumped his knee a little harder. "*Fishing* rod, babe. Start talking."

He chuckled softly, took a quick bite of ham and beans and then got down to business. "Okay, let's see, how do I describe ol' Bessie. She's—"

"You *named* your fishing rod?"

He smiled fondly. "Actually, my granddad did. It was his originally. He bought it for himself as a gift when he was promoted to vice president of his company."

"If it was a gift to mark such a big event it must have been one heck of a fancy rod."

Admiration and affection shone from his eyes. "The best. A Thomas and Thomas split-cane fly fishing rod. The Rolls-Royce of fishing rods world over. Six pieces of hand-selected split cane glued together by master craftsmen to create the unique hexagonal shape of the bamboo rod."

"Sounds exotic. What color is it?"

"Ah, that's one of the things I like best about the bamboo fishing rods as opposed to the new graphite ones. The color. There's just something about metallic green or blue or pink, for crying out loud, that disturbs the natural picture when I'm fishing. Bamboo rods range in color from dark gold to light gold, but they're all tones of their original self.'' A fond smile turned his lips. ''Bessie is light gold with a soft patina. Beautiful. A pleasure to hold. A pleasure to watch work against the forest's foliage or the river's water or the blue sky.''

He spoke about the rod as if it was its own entity. Something with a will of its own. A soul of its own. ''Did your granddad give it to you when he got too old to use it?''

He laughed. ''Granddad never got too old to use it. He and Grandma lived beside one of the best fishing streams in the Smokies, and he fished right up to the day he quit breathing.''

It made her sad to think of him losing someone so dear to him. But she was glad the man had left him something to remember him by. ''Did he leave it to you, then?''

''Nope. My grandmother gave it to my dad, said he should have it since he'd spent so much time fishing with his father. But Dad already had a Thomas and Thomas. A ten-year wedding anniversary gift from my mom. So when I was sixteen, and old enough to take care of it, according to my father, my dad gave it to me.''

His expression softened as though he was remembering the special day. The special gift. ''I can still picture Granddad using it when we all went fishing together. He had several rods, of course. Rods that loaded faster—which just means you can cast faster and that the line goes through the air in faster, tighter loops,'' he explained. "But it was the split-cane Thomas and Thomas he always used. Always.''

He stopped, took a bite of mushy ham and beans, his expression nostalgic. A man remembering old times. "Granddad always said no one gave him the thrill old Bessie did. She loads slow, he used to say, but no one sends the line dancing through the air more gracefully than she.'' His smile hitched up at the corners. "And he was right.''

Her heart squeezed. Old skills and old traditions being passed down from one generation to the next in a place where the world's speed and efficiency gave way to sentiment and grace. "You're a lucky man, Mr. Smith, to have such memories.'' She'd never known any of her grandparents. And while she'd continually hoped her father would show up for her birthdays—not to bring her a gift, but to wish her well, to celebrate with her mother and her, he never had.

"Yes. I am lucky.'' Another shadow flitted across his face.

She cocked her head, studying him. The first shadow had come and gone so quickly she thought she might have imagined it. But she was sure of this one. His grandfather was gone, of course, there would be no new memories there. But, barring a young death or fatal accident, the father should still be alive. So why did he look as if those times were over for good?

And then it clicked. "Oh, God. It was in the plane, wasn't it? Your fishing rod. Bessie."

"No, it—" He shook his head quickly. Too quickly.

She stopped the denial before he'd finished it. She knew he was lying. "Don't lie to me. It was, wasn't it?" She locked her gaze on his, demanding the truth from him. She was tired of men lying to her, even if it was to make her feel better, and she sensed that was Smith's only motive for the lie he was trying to pass off now.

He hesitated, frowning, but then he gave his head a short succinct nod. "Yes, it was. But I don't want you to feel guilty about it. Or bad about it. Life happens."

How could she not feel bad? Or guilty? Yes, something under the dash had caught fire. Not her fault. And there had been damned little choice in landing sites. Not her fault, either. But still, in the end, she was the one who had crashed the plane. She set her lunch down, her stomach turning. "I am so, so sorry."

He wrapped his arm around her and pulled her against his side for a comforting hug. "I said no feeling bad. I guarantee both my grandfather and my dad would have told you the only two important things in that plane were the two people in it. You saved those, that's all that matters."

"But still—"

"Still nothing. Like I said, life happens. Stop

thinking about it.'' He gave her a comforting squeeze.

She placed her hand on his chest and leaned into him, soaking up his heat, trying to offer *him* some comfort. "I'm still sorry."

He chuckled softly and gave her another hug. "I appreciate it."

She should have pulled away from him then, but… His heat, his strength, his…everything felt too good. And he didn't let her go, so she stayed. Just for one second more, she promised herself.

But one second turned into two and then five. Subtly, the comforting embrace changed. His hand stroked up her back. Up and then back down, settling at her waist, his fingers gently flexing there as though measuring the curve. Or savoring it.

The air around them shifted, becoming heavier, hotter…more restless. She looked up at his face.

He stared down at her, his brown-eyed gaze intense, focused. Sensual.

Her breath caught in her throat. Heat and need slid through her. A dangerous heat. An unwanted need. Everything about Smith intrigued her—enticed her—but he was a *man*, for the love of God. And she wasn't doing men anymore. And just because it felt so damned good to be in his arms didn't change that.

But, oh, it made it hard to remember.

His gaze dropped to her lips, narrowing, heating.

A hot, greedy tingle shot through her. She'd bet her last dollar Smith could make a woman forget her *name* with those lips, forget anything that needed more brain power than pure, raw primal response. Anything like resolve. Which was exactly why she couldn't let those chiseled, sensual lips anywhere near her.

But, oh, she wanted to let them near. Wanted to feel them against her own, feel them nibble over her tingling flesh.

He lowered his head, his intent clear, his breath whispering over her cheeks.

She held her breath, want and need making the blood rush through her veins, past pains screaming at her to run now while the running was good. Kiss? Run? She pushed back just before his lips touched hers. "I can't do this."

He didn't try to stop her withdrawal, but his hand remained on her waist, his gaze locked on hers, sensual promise shining from brown depths. "Sure you can. All you have to do is close your eyes and think sweet thoughts. I'll do the rest."

Something hot and liquid melted inside her. If she didn't do something fast, she was a gonner. She shot off the porch, shaking her head. "It's not that easy. I'm starting a new life here, remember?" She probably would have sounded a lot more convincing if she wasn't so breathless, if her voice hadn't been quite so weak.

"I remember you mentioning it, yes. What does that have to do with this?" His heavy-lidded gaze tracked her like a heat-seeking missile.

She drew a deep breath, pulled her shoulders back

and pushed the thought of just how exciting Smith's kiss might be right out of her head. "It has everything to do with this because the cornerstone of my new life is my resolve to exclude all *men* from it."

His lips thinned, but his heated gaze didn't cool an ounce. "Does this have anything to do with your ex, by any chance?"

She tipped her chin up. "Yes. Mr. Now-That-You've-Spent-the-Last-Four-Years-of-Your-Life-Cooking-and-Cleaning-for-Me-I'm Running-Off-with-Another-Woman Jerk has a lot to do with it. But—"

"He was only one man, Winnie. You can't banish the entire male population because of one jerk." He came off the steps like a panther on the prowl, his muscles flexing smoothly, his stride long and slow as he strode toward her.

She swallowed hard and started backing up, doing her best to keep a safe distance between them. Struggling to keep her resolve strong. "Actually, my darling ex wasn't the first man to promise me sunshine and roses and leave me with nothing but tears and bank debts. My father set the pattern long before I met Tucker Taylor, remember?"

He shrugged those big, wide shoulders. "I'm not your ex, Winnie. Or your father. And I'm not promising you anything but a kiss. A simple, straightforward kiss."

Her mouth went dry. "Why do I suspect that a man who waxes so passionately about a fishing rod, for the love of Pete, doesn't have the slightest clue how to deliver a *simple* kiss.'' She'd bet her wings it had been years since Mr. Smith had delivered a kiss that stopped short of naked skin and soft, ecstatic cries.

He smiled, slow and sexy. ''What if I promise to keep it short and sweet? Will you stop backing away then?''

She laughed, a little hysterically. ''Do you even *remember* the last time you gave someone a short, sweet kiss?''

His lips twisted wryly. ''No, but—''

''See, that's my problem. And—'' She stumbled into something hard and rough and absolutely immobile. A tree. And before she could regain her footing and skirt around it, Smith was half a step in front of her, blocking her in.

His hard body towered over her, his heat soaking into her.

She swallowed hard. ''This isn't a good idea.''

He leaned closer, reaching over her head with one arm, leaning against the tree Rocky-style. ''It's a cold, cruel world out there, Winnie. A man gets lucky enough to have something sweet and joyful come along, he's a fool to walk away without a taste. That's all I want. A little taste.''

Her heart squeezed. ''Is that me? Sweet?''

He raised a single brow. ''You doubt it?''

She looked away. It had been a long time since anyone had considered her…well, a long time since anyone had considered her anything. Except maybe the housekeeper.

Which was *why* she was banishing men from her life, she reminded herself sternly.

But her lips, her traitorous lips, wouldn't stop tingling. And her mind, her feeble, weak mind, wouldn't stop thinking how wonderful it would be to be touched, kissed by a man who'd noticed her enough to think she was sweet. *This isn't Tucker,* a tiny voice in the back of her head whispered. *This is a man who cares about the things around him. He even loves his fishing rod, for pity's sake. And right now he's looking at you like you're the most desirable thing on earth.*

Tucker had *never* looked at her like that. And it wasn't as if she was signing her life over to the man. Just a few seconds. What could one short, sweet kiss possibly hurt?

She looked back to him, her gaze locking on to his.

It was the only invitation he needed. He settled his hand at her waist and dipped his head, his lips closing over hers.

Warm.

Soft.

Achingly tender.

Heat and need slid through her. Had she ever been kissed so...reverently? She ran her hands up his sides, over his chest. He felt so good. Hard. Hot. She leaned closer, trying to increase the pressure of his lips.

He rocked back just enough to keep the kiss innocent. And then he pulled his lips from hers, his fingers flexing restlessly at the soft curve of her waist, as though stopping the kiss was the last thing he wanted to do.

Her fingers dug into his sides. She didn't want the moment to stop, either. Not when she was just starting to feel like someone special. It was far too rare an event to just let slip away before she'd tasted it fully. She raised her gaze to his. "You're not going to stop are you?"

His nostrils flared with desire. "If you want me to stop at 'short and sweet,' I am."

She ran a hand up his ribs, drinking in the hard feel of him, kissing the last bit of her resistance goodbye. "Short and sweet was...wonderful. Now I want to see what's next."

His dark brown gaze edged toward midnight. "Absolutely." His voice was low, rough, as he pulled her close and dipped his head.

His lips closed over hers. Not sweet this time, but as raw and primal as she'd expected his kisses to be. His lips moved over hers, seeking her sharpest response, demanding her sharpest response. His hands stroked up her sides boldly, exploring her every curve, her every hill.

Desire shook her.

His hands cradled her head, tilting it just so, giving him maximum access, his tongue stroking hers.

Her fingers dug into him, pulling him closer, savoring the feel of his hard body. Savoring his heat.

His hips bumped hers, the hard ridge of his arousal nudging her belly. A soft, needy moan vibrated against her lips as his fingers threaded restlessly through her hair, rubbing the strands as if testing its texture or trying to memorize its feel. He pulled his lips away, his gaze studying the dark curls twining around his fingers. And then he looked to her face, studying it with equal fervor. "Beautiful," he whispered.

Her breath caught in her throat. Her heart thumped. She wanted to believe the words—but she didn't. Disappointment skittered through her, and she looked away, embarrassment heating her cheeks.

He tipped her chin back to him, the warmth of his finger against her cheek. "You don't believe me."

She grimaced. "My mother always said I was smart and capable. My dad told me I was adventurous, daring even. Tucker, on a good day, called me cute. I think beauty is probably beyond me. And if we're going to do this, I want it to be honest. I don't want you making things up because you think it's what I want to hear. Or need to hear."

His eyes narrowed to thin, brown bands as he locked them on her with unnerving intensity. "I'm sorry your parents didn't let you know you were beautiful. As for your ex, we've already established he's a jerk. Now we know he's also blind. Lastly, you want honesty? Here's some for you. While I'm the man standing in front of you, I don't want you thinking about that bastard. I want you thinking about me. And *I* think you're beautiful." His lips claimed hers.

Hot.

Hard.

Demanding.

Joy shot through her. With his lips devouring hers, his hands moving over her with greedy homage, she *felt* beautiful. Beautiful and special and wanted. Every coherent thought fled. Everything but the feel of him, the taste of him, the magic of the moment.

A steady, throbbing roar echoed in her ears. The earth seemed to swirl around them. The earth shook beneath her feet.

Suddenly he tore his mouth from hers and looked over his shoulder.

Her lips felt cold, bereft without his touch. But the roar still sounded in her ears, the earth still seemed to shake. And then she realized those sensations weren't internal. They were external. The roar turned into a deafening whop, whop, whop. The swirling air turned into a miniwindstorm. And the earth shook harder beneath their feet. She looked over his shoulder, in the same direction he was looking.

A giant, black helicopter hovered against the blue sky. No, it wasn't hovering. It was lowering steadily to the ground.

Rescue had arrived.

Chapter Nine

Winnie sat in the back of the big, noisy helicopter between two of the men who'd rescued them. Cash Ryan and Talon Redhorse, if she remembered the hurried introductions correctly. Cash, a handsome man with a fit, athletic body and no-nonsense expression sat on her left. And Talon, a Native American with long, shiny black hair flowing over his shoulders and an inscrutable expression on his sharply chiseled features sat on her right. Both men and the pilot, Griffon Tyner, were dressed in camouflage, which made her think her rescue had come at the hands of some branch of the military. Their quick departure from the small cabin had certainly been carried out with military precision.

And now they were on their way back to Henry's. She should be elated. All in all she and Smith had been lucky. They hadn't been badly injured in the crash, and they'd experienced no real hardships since. They'd never been cold or hungry or thirsty. No bears had eaten them. So while she might have wished rescue had waited another five minutes— okay, half an hour or so—to arrive, she should be thrilled they were heading home in good shape. But the only reaction she could muster right now was a disquieting sense of unease.

Something was wrong with this rescue picture. While she sat in the back, where she would assume the rescued parties would sit, Smith was up front with the pilot. And while neither Smith nor the men who had rescued them had acknowledged knowing each other, they had moved almost as a unit from the moment the helicopter had landed. Working side by side with the men in camo, Smith had helped grab the survival gear, put the cabin back the way they'd found it and ushered them into the helicopter.

And now Smith was up front having an intense talk with the pilot over their headsets. If the pilot was debriefing anyone on the crash shouldn't it be *her,* the pilot of the plane? She leaned toward the soldier on her left and pitched her voice above the roar of the helicopter blades. "Is there another headset available? I think I should be the one talking to the pilot."

"It looks like they're having a private conversation, ma'am. When they're done I'll get you a set."

Her uneasiness increased, sending a slow chill up her spine. To her knowledge men who didn't know each other didn't have big-time private conversations. She shifted in her seat. She wanted to know what was going on, and she wanted to know now. She reached forward and snatched the headset from Smith's head.

His gaze snapped to hers.

"What's going on?" she hollered.

He grimaced, but didn't try to retrieve his headset. He merely grabbed another one from the floor at his feet and put those on.

She quickly put on the set she held. "What's going on," she repeated. "Do you know these people?" Her stomach clenched. She wasn't sure why it would be bad if he knew them, but she felt instinctively it would be.

His lips thinned to a narrow, unhappy line and she could all but see the wheels turning in his head as he formulated his answer.

"You're going to have to tell her, Rand." The pilot's voice crackled over the silent headphones. "Nieto's men landed in the lower forty-eight two days ago. If the FBI doesn't nab them, it won't take them long to track her here. She needs to know what's going on. And we need whatever information she has on Tucker. Now."

Nieto's men? Tucker? *What* was going on here? But more important… She pinned her gaze on Smith. "Who the hell is Rand?"

He grimaced, his gaze flitting away. When he

looked back, his brows were pulled low in a dark frown. "I'm Rand. Rand Michaels. Bob Smith is a cover name."

A cover name? She'd heard of photojournalists using different names. But only when they were working a story. The sense of uneasiness turned to dread. "Why were you using a cover name with me? And who are these people?"

He tipped his head toward the pilot. "Griff is my boss."

That feeling of dread got worse. "Your boss? Do you work for a magazine or something? I had the impression you were freelance."

"Not exactly."

She narrowed her eyes on him. "What do you mean not exactly?"

His lips pressed into a thin, hard line. "I'm not a freelance photographer, Winnie. I'm a mercenary. Tyner runs the mercenary band I work for. Freedom Rings."

"A mercenary band?" Dear God, what had she wandered into?

Smith gave his head a single, succinct nod, his expression grim. "You needn't look like you're about to be slaughtered and tossed out of the plane. We're the good guys."

"The good guys?" She sounded as stunned as she felt. "The good guys in what?"

"The search for Tucker Taylor."

She raised a brow. "Is he missing?"

Excitement sparked in his eyes. "Do you know where he is?"

"No. But I'm sure the CIA does. They keep track of their retired agents, don't they?"

His black scowl returned full force. "Only the ones that retire in the conventional manner."

Confusion pounded in her head. "What does that mean?"

"It means Tucker decided to create his own retirement package. He ran off with fifty million of Uncle Sam's dollars, and the CIA wants to talk to him about it. They're the ones looking for him."

The words congregated in her head, but they didn't make sense. Tucker running off with fifty million dollars? Fifty million dollars of Uncle Sam's money? No way. And even if he had, how would Rand Michaels, *mercenary,* know about it? Something wasn't right here.

She narrowed her gaze on Smith or Michaels or whoever he was. "How do *you* know the CIA is looking for Tucker?"

"Because I'm working for them."

"*What?* You just told me you were a *mercenary.* And that you worked for that guy." She pointed a finger at their pilot.

He gave his head that single nod. "I am and I do, but sometimes the CIA hires outside help. This is one of those times."

The CIA hired mercenaries? Now there was a comforting thought. She held her hands up. "Stop.

This is too confusing. I'm not answering one more question until you tell me *exactly* what is going on.''

He hesitated for a moment as if he wasn't sure where to start. Finally he said, ''A while back the Colombian government asked the U.S. to help them bring down one of their major drug lords, Miguel Nieto. Since Nieto is responsible for a third of the Colombian drugs that filter into our country, the U.S. agreed.''

''Enter the CIA.''

''Yes. Several plans were looked at, everything from full military attacks to the more subtle plans the CIA is so famous for. In the end, an arms sting seemed to be the surest ticket. Nieto has a big army, and he likes them armed to the teeth. Rifles. Small munitions. Stingers. You name it, Nieto wants a bunkerful.''

''Is this where Tucker comes in? And you?''

He nodded. ''Tucker had done several arms stings in the past, so he was the man the CIA picked to head the mission. But they needed one more man to work the negotiations with Tucker, and soldiers to carry out the final arrests. They called Freedom Rings and requested me for the second negotiator and several men for the arrests.''

''They requested you? I take it they know you.''

He nodded. ''Before I joined Freedom Rings I worked for the CIA.''

Her stomach clenched. ''A CIA operative. And now a mercenary. How peachy. Why do I think this story only gets uglier from here?''

He went on, ignoring her sarcasm. "The Colombian operation was supposed to be simple. Tucker and I lure Nieto into an arms deal. Then on the day of the buy, Freedom Rings men swarm in and arrest Nieto and his men. After which, the arms and the fifty million Nieto was paying for them were supposed to be sent back to America."

"I take it that didn't happen."

"The deal went smooth as glass until our guys swarmed in for the arrests, then all hell broke loose. Several explosions went off in the surrounding jungle, making our support troops think we were surrounded by guerrillas. The neat, clean attack we had planned turned to chaos. And during that chaos Tucker disappeared—along with the fifty million dollars."

She shook her head. "No way. Tucker wouldn't have stolen that money. He isn't like that. The man's a womanizing jerk, yes. But a thief? No. He's one of the good guys, for pity's sake. One of Nieto's men must have gotten away with the money."

Michaels shook his head. "Nieto and two of his captains did manage to elude capture. And they were the first men we looked at for the missing money— despite Tucker's suspicious disappearance. But it didn't take long before we heard Nieto was looking for the money as hard and not nearly as nicely as we are. Tucker's our man, Winnie."

Her stomach turned. It had been bad enough when she'd discovered Tucker hadn't loved her, that he was running off with another woman. But this…good God. Had she ever even known the real Tucker Taylor at all? Had she spent four years of her life with…what? A mirage?

She swallowed hard, fearing the answer to her next question. "So what does all this have to do with me? Why are you *here* looking for Tucker?"

The corners of his lips pulled down. "We're here because the only lead we have on Tucker is you. We thought you might be his accomplice."

"His accomplice? He had an accomplice?" The story got more confusing by the moment.

Michaels nodded. "It was obvious when we found the explosive devices that had gone off in the jungle that someone had been there helping him. The charges weren't set on timers, they'd been detonated by remote control. Someone had been close enough to watch the operation and then set the devices off at the most opportune time."

"And you thought that someone was *me?*" Indignation sent a reviving jolt of anger through her. "I've never so much as gotten a parking ticket! And the CIA has to know I've never left the country. They did check that didn't they?"

"They knew you'd never left the country under your own name, yes. But Tucker certainly would have known how to acquire a fake ID for you."

She shook her head. "I don't believe this. I'm *divorced* from the man. They do know I'm divorced from Tucker, don't they?"

"They know."

"Then why— Wait a minute. Did Tucker steal this money before or after our divorce?"

"After."

Relief slid through her. "Then I repeat, *why* are they looking at me? Why on earth would the CIA think I would help my *ex*-husband steal fifty million dollars?"

"The divorce could have been part of the plan. A ploy meant to do exactly what you just implied. Take our eyes off you. That would give Tucker a safe place to drop the money while he made his getaway. Then later, when the search cooled down, you could quietly slip away and meet up with him."

She rolled her eyes. "That is the lamest escape plan I have ever heard. And did it ever occur to them to wonder why, if I had fifty million dollars sitting around somewhere, I'd be struggling to pay my bills? I'm assuming they looked at my credit report. God knows, they seemed to have looked at everything else." Her voice rose with each word. The thought of Tucker sitting pretty with his new honey while she struggled to pay old debts—many of which *he'd* incurred—made her mad enough to spit nails.

Michaels's voice crackled over her headset. "They looked at your finances, yes. But if Tucker had wanted the CIA to overlook you, having it seem as if you were in a financial crunch was the perfect touch. After all, as you just pointed out, who would suspect a woman of helping to steal fifty million dollars if she was struggling to pay her bills?"

She curled her lip. "You and your colleagues have twisted little minds, you know that?"

Dark shadows filled his eyes. "It comes with the territory. You spend your days with the seedy underbelly of society, sooner or later you start thinking like them."

She shook her head. "Which is why instead of knocking on my door like respectable human beings and asking me what I knew about my husband's disappearance with fifty million of Uncle Sam's dollars you decided to insinuate yourself in my life as a charter client. And you thought…what? That in the two hours it would take me to fly you to the lodge you'd be able to get me to relax and chat enough that I might give up some important fact that would tip you off as to my guilt? Or maybe even Tucker's whereabouts?" It seemed like a huge order for a two-hour flight. And then a sudden, horrible thought occurred to her. "Oh, God, did you plan the crash?" Her stomach twisted at the thought, but she knew it was within the CIA's capabilities.

"No!" The denial was quick and emphatic. "Why on earth would I do that? I'd have a hard time getting information out of you if we were both dead."

"You might not have realized how hard it would be to find a landing spot once the fire on the plane started. And having me in a secluded spot, dependent on you for survival would make your job a whole lot easier."

Anger sparked in his eyes. "I've been working

undercover a long time, Winnie. Getting information from suspects is my specialty. I'm damned good at it. I don't need to drag people into desperate seclusion to do my job. I might very well have gotten what information I needed from you in that two-hour flight. But if I hadn't, there would have been more flights. Until we became friends. Until you were comfortable enough to give me the information I needed.''

She shook her head. ''No, there wouldn't have been. I don't fly charters, I fly cargo.''

''Do you think it was an accident I showed up to be chartered on the one day out of the year when Henry was short charter pilots? It was all planned, Winnie. I was to fly with you that one day, and if I didn't get the information I needed, I'd call Henry's the next day, extol your flying ability and request you take me somewhere else. Just you, no one else. Henry is a smart businessman. He would have arranged it.''

There was a cold determination in his voice that sent a chill down her spine. He seemed a totally different man from the one who'd taken her fishing. The one who'd...dear God. Pain slashed through her. She looked to the pilot. ''Would you mind giving us a few moments of privacy, Mr. Tyner?''

Tyner spared her a quick glance over his shoulder, but then he turned back to his controls and removed his headset.

She leveled her gaze back on Michaels, her heart squeezing. ''Is that what the kiss was about? I wasn't giving you enough information on Tucker. You thought a little seduction might—''

''*No.*'' Fire blazed in his eyes. ''I was off the clock then. What went on between you and me from the day I took you fishing until the helicopter picked us up had nothing to do with this case.'' He plowed angry fingers through his short hair. ''For crying out loud, I knew you were innocent from the moment I saw that damned makeup strewn on the ground. And even though I still needed to discover what information you had on Tucker, I decided it could wait. I was enjoying your company. I was enjoying you. The last thing I wanted to think about was the damned job. Or Tucker.''

His anger at her accusation sounded real. His sincerity when he claimed he'd cared about her sounded real. But the man made his living by making people believe what came out of his mouth. And he'd made no bones about the fact he was good at his job. She shook her head in disgust. ''Yeah. Right.'' She yanked her headphones off and looked away, embarrassment and pain and anger slicing through her.

Forty minutes ago she'd been reveling in his embrace. Reveling in the feel of him, the taste of him. Reveling in the way he made her feel special.

She shook her head in disgust. She was *such* an idiot.

Would she *never* learn?

Rand turned away from Winnie and stared out the helo's windshield at the blue sky before him. The

bright sunshine hurt his eyes and sent a stab of irritation through him. Dark skies and a booming
thunderstorm would feel good about now. But no,
like everything else on this mission, even nature was
thumbing its nose at him.

He dug his finger into his eyes, wondering how
in blazes he was going to fix this mess. He mentally
shook his head. What the hell had he been thinking?
Kissing Winnie Mae Taylor. It was one thing to allow himself to soak in her sweetness, her goodness,
to pretend he was an average guy named Bob Smith
and that life was simple and wonderful and bright.
It was his own little fantasy. Everyone had one. But
the minute he'd put his lips on hers, he'd pushed his
fantasy into her reality.

Unfair.

And yet, he hadn't been able to resist.

It was as if something inside him had snapped
when she'd snuggled against him. The fantasy
hadn't been enough anymore. He'd wanted to taste
the real thing. And there she'd been in his arms. All
warm and soft with what seemed to be the same
loneliness, the same wistful longing for human contact in her eyes that he felt in his own empty chest.
And he'd had to have her. For just a moment.

And now she was paying for his moment of self-
ishness.

He scrubbed a hand down his face, fatigue and
regret pounding in his head. How the hell was he
going to fix this?

Long before he had an answer, they arrived at Henry's, the helicopter setting down with a soft thump. Before Griffon had even shut the engine off, Winnie bolted, crawling over Cash and escaping onto the tarmac. Heading as fast as her legs would carry her, she sprinted toward Henry and several other men, both young and old who had no doubt gathered outside to await the Freedom Rings helicopter the minute Griff had called to say they'd found Winnie and her passenger.

Rand piled out of the helo with the rest of the Freedom Rings crew. While Cash and Talon headed toward the small building that housed the airport's lobby and maintenance quarters, he and Griffon headed toward the little reunion where Winnie was receiving back slaps and hugs and glad-you're-back-safe-and-sound welcomes.

"We still need her, you know?" Griffon commented as the helicopter blades slowed to a slow whomp, whomp, whomp over their heads. "She might think she doesn't know where Tucker is, but she undoubtedly has information that will help locate him…even if she doesn't realize it. We'll have to question her. And until Nieto's men are caught she's in danger. She'll need protection. It'll be easier if she's cooperating."

"No kidding?" Sarcasm dripped from Rand's words.

Griff stopped, bringing them both to a halt. He studied Rand for a moment, his gaze hard and assessing. "Is there a problem here I should know about? Something she felt she had to talk to you privately about, perhaps?''

Rand gritted his teeth. "No. Everything's fine."

Griff cocked a challenging brow. "Is that right? You wouldn't mind telling me then what *exactly* was going on in those woods between you two when we dropped in?"

"What was going on in those woods is none of your business."

Griff took a slow, deep, temper-curbing breath. "There is a reason, you know, why getting involved with your target is a bad idea. I can see the temptation, she's a beautiful woman. But—"

Rand slashed his hand through the air. "Skip the lecture. I know the rules. I know the reasons. I screwed up. I'll do what I can to smooth things over."

Griff gave him another long look, but finally gave his head a short, curt nod. "Okay. But do it soon. Life will be a lot easier—and safer—for everyone if she's cooperating."

Like he didn't know that. The only question was, how was he going to achieve that happy goal? Without another word he strode away from Griff and over to the group clustered around Winnie.

He watched as Winnie pulled herself from Henry's hug, regret and apology furrowing her brow as she looked at the old man. "Henry, I don't know what to say. I wrecked the plane. There was a fire under the dash and there was nowhere to land." She wrung her hands. Tears gathered in her eyes.

Rand prepared to step in. He wasn't going to let her lose her job over this. Not if he could help it.

But Henry settled his arm over her shoulders in a fatherly fashion, his face a mask of gruff reassurance. "Don't you worry about it. You and Smith are in one piece, that's all that counts. As for the plane, what do you think I've been paying that insurance man the past twenty years for? It's about time I got a new plane for my money. God knows, for what I've paid in, I should have an entire new fleet on my tarmac."

Winnie chuckled softly, the sound watery and weak as she hugged him back. "If they don't cover the entire cost of the replacement, Henry, you let me know. I'll make up the difference. I promise. You can take it out of my pay. If—" uncertainty flashed across her face "—if I still have a job."

Henry shot her an impatient scowl. "Of course you have a job. What kind of talk is that? And you quit worrying about the damned plane. That's my business."

Rand breathed a little sigh of relief. At least he hadn't totally screwed up her life. She still had her job. And he'd make sure Henry didn't suffer any ill effects from the crash, either.

Winnie gave Henry a quick hug. "Thanks, Henry. What about the FAA? Did you let them know we've been found, or should I give them a call?"

Henry shook his head. "I called the minute Mr. Tyner radioed in that they'd found you. The search has been officially called off. They'll send someone down tomorrow to talk to you, to get the crash site, etcetera, etcetera. Until then the only thing you need to worry about is getting some rest. And seeing a doctor. I want you checked out. Both of you.'' Henry lifted his gaze to Rand's.

''I'm fine, Henry,'' Rand said. ''No need for a doctor. But Winnie could use one.'' He tipped his head toward the bandage on her arm.

Henry looked to her arm, his brows crashing together in concern. ''Well for Pete's sake, I was so glad to see you I didn't notice the bandage. How bad is it?''

Winnie shot Rand a nasty look, then turned back to Henry, smoothing her features into a reassuring expression. ''Not bad. Just a little cut. I'll see a doctor tomorrow if you want. I promise. But not now. Right now I need to fly.'' She dropped a quick kiss on the older man's cheek and strode away before he could protest.

Rand quickly fell into step beside her. ''You can't go flying. You're injured. Tired. You're in no shape to—''

She lengthened her step, pulling away from him, ignoring him completely.

He took one long stride, grabbed her arm and pulled her around.

She spun on him like a fighting tiger. ''Back off, Michaels. Find a phone and tell your CIA buddies I didn't have anything to do with Tucker's little scam in Colombia. And then get your butt on a plane and get out of my life.'' She jerked out of his grip and stalked away.

He started after her again, but a hand grabbed his own arm, pulling him around.

Griffon shook his head at him. "Let her go. She looks like she needs to blow off a little steam."

"She shouldn't be doing it flying."

"Maybe not, but her other option seems to be going one-on-one with you. And I don't think that's going to get either of you anywhere right now." He rocked back on his heels, his gaze meeting Rand's head on. "If it will make things easier, I can put Cash in your place. There's no need for subterfuge now. And she might be more cooperative with someone else."

Rand narrowed his eyes on his boss. "You're not putting anyone in my place."

Griff raised a knowing brow. "It's like that, is it?"

Hell, no, it wasn't like that. It could never be "like that." Hearth, home and happily-ever-after weren't in his future. But he didn't want Cash or any other man anywhere near her. She was *his* responsibility. And he would damn well take care of her. He shot Griff a warning scowl. "It's not 'like' anything. But it's my mess. I'll clean it up."

Griff's lips thinned unhappily, but he tipped his head in curt acknowledgment. "Fine. But do it fast. The clock's ticking."

Chapter Ten

Rand stood on the tarmac and watched Winnie disappear into an aluminum-sided hangar with a giant sliding door. He didn't like the idea of her flying, but maybe Griff was right. Maybe if she blew off a little steam she'd settle down enough to talk to him. He turned away from Griff and caught Henry's eye. "Where the hell does she fly when she's upset, Henry?" He didn't like the idea of her being out of his sight. Even for a little while.

"That's her hangar she just walked into. She's getting out the *Angry Bullet.*" The old man pointed to the sky above. "Reckon she'll just be flying overhead."

Well, there was a break. A damned small one. But the way this case was going he'd take what he could get. Just as he finished the thought, he heard her engine kick into life with a low, powerful growl.

It revved a few times and then a plane was taxiing out of the hangar she'd disappeared into. He caught his breath. It was one mean-looking machine. A low-winged tail dragger, its sleek nose pointed arrogantly into the air while its black-gray-and-red paint job made it look exactly like what the name scrawled across the nose implied—an angry bullet streaking through the sky.

Just the kind of machine a tired, injured pilot could get herself in trouble in if she wasn't damned careful. His gut clenching, he watched the plane taxi over the tarmac, pick up speed on the short runway and hurtle itself into the air with an earsplitting roar just as it came to the end of the pavement.

Henry leaned close, pitching his voice above the sound. "Ever been to an air show?"

He shook his head. "Never had the pleasure."

"Hang on to your hat, then. You're about to be initiated by one of the best."

He wasn't certain whether that was a good thing or a bad thing as the *Angry Bullet* rocketed toward the sky. Up and up and up it climbed, the screaming engine getting a little quieter with every foot of altitude, the plane's silhouette diminishing with the sound. When the plane was about the size of a silver dollar it seemed to stall, its engine quieting to a rough whisper as it hung in the air as if suspended from the prop. And then the aircraft tipped to the side, pivoting on a wingtip and headed straight for the ground, nose first, the whispering engine getting louder and louder until it was screaming like a banshee.

It looked like a pretty straightforward maneuver, but he held his breath, anyway. And when she didn't pull out of the dive as soon as he would have liked, his heart pounded harder than her prop. Simple maneuver or not, she was tired. Her reflexes would be slow. And at the speed she was flying toward the earth if she didn't do something soon…

A cold sweat broke out on his skin. "Dammit, Winnie, pull out of it," he whispered to himself, clenching his fists.

At the last possible second the plane pulled out of the dive, its landing gear brushing the waist deep grass of the field in front of them.

He breathed a sigh of relief. But it was short-lived. She was climbing again. Up and up and up with a couple of snap rolls just to keep everyone's attention. When she hit the top of her climb this time the engine whispered to a halt. The silence was deafening. And then she was dropping toward the ground nose first again, this time in a series of spins that left him breathless. And then flat out scared as she kept spinning long after he thought she should have pulled out of the maneuver.

At the last possible moment the plane quit spinning, but it was still heading silently for the ground. Suddenly the engine coughed to life and finally, *finally* Winnie pulled out of the dive just short of the earth, her wheels once again kissing the grass.

He stabbed his fingers through his hair. What the hell did she think she was doing? Or was pretending to fly the damned plane into the ground just part of the show? He glanced quickly at Henry and Griff, both aviation aficionados, to see how they were taking it.

Neither of them were wearing isn't-this-exciting grins. In fact, they both looked a little tense.

His gut pulled a little tighter, and a few more beads of sweat broke out on his skin as she pushed the plane through several more tricky maneuvers.

She climbed high again, and he held his breath. What ugly stunt did she have up her sleeve this time? Suddenly the plane seemed to trip over its nose and then go tumbling nose over tail, wing tip over tip. He gasped, his heart stopping. This didn't look like a planned maneuver at all. It looked like she was tumbling out of control. He rushed forward a few steps as if to put himself in a better position to catch the plane should it fall out of the sky. Like that would do anyone a damned bit of good.

Henry stepped up and touched his arm. "Easy boy, it's a Lomcevak. It's supposed to look like the plane is reeling drunkenly, but it's not. She's in control."

He turned to Griff. "Does it look to you like she's in control of that plane?"

Griff's lips pulled down and he tipped his head fatalistically. "As long as she's a hundred feet above the ground, don't worry about her. It's that last five feet that will kill her." His lips pressed into a tight, unhappy line. "Unfortunately, she seems to be flirting with that five feet more often than necessary."

She sure as hell was. How many times had she dragged her wheels through the grass? But was she pulling out of the maneuvers late because she was mad and pushing the envelope or because she was tired and her reflexes were slow? Or, God forbid was she trying to scare him? He'd hurt her. Giving him a good scare might be her way of getting even.

Acid poured into his gut. He turned to Henry. "How long does she usually stay up, Henry?"

"She only carries enough fuel for about fifteen minutes. She'll be down soon."

Thank God. His nerves were stretched tighter than a piano wire. He watched as she pushed the plane through a few loops and a tight barrel roll, then headed for the runway. His heart slowed down, and a thread of relief snaked through him. It looked as if she was calling it quits. And not a moment too soon, he'd had all the excitement he could take for the day.

Suddenly she did a snap roll, turning the plane upside down with crisp precision and roaring down the runway toward them. The engine screamed, the plane's black tail stretched toward the ground, her clear canopy a mere ten feet from the hard, black pavement.

His heart kicked into double time. Anger streaked through him. If she was pushing the envelope out of anger, she needed to have her license jerked. And if she was getting even with him, he was going to wring her neck.

She sped past them, her long curly tresses hanging down, brushing the curved glass of the canopy, her smug gaze boring into him like a couple of weapon-grade lasers.

The knot in his gut pulled a little tighter. His anger spiked a little higher. If she made it out of that plane in one piece, he was going to kill her.

Another snap roll once she passed them and she was upright again. Upright and climbing to a safe altitude.

He unclenched his fists and sucked in a full breath of air.

She flew the plane through a quick half loop and headed for the runway. This time she landed, her wheels gently setting down on the pavement.

Rand watched her taxi the plane up the runway and over to her hangar, anger pouring over him.

Griffon stepped up beside him. "It might be a good idea if you count to ten before you go storming after her."

He locked gazes with Griff and counted.

The Silhouette Reader Service™ — Here's how it works:

Accepting your 2 free books and gift places you under no obligation to buy anything. You may keep the books and gift and return the shipping statement marked "cancel." If you do not cancel, about a month later we'll send you 6 additional books and bill you just $3.99 each in the U.S., or $4.74 each in Canada, plus 25¢ shipping & handling per book and applicable taxes if any.* That's the complete price and — compared to cover prices of $4.75 each in the U.S. and $5.75 each in Canada — it's quite a bargain! You may cancel at any time, but if you choose to continue, every month we'll send you 6 more books, which you may either purchase at the discount price or return to us and cancel your subscription. *Terms and prices subject to change without notice. Sales tax applicable in N.Y. Canadian residents will be charged applicable provincial taxes and GST. Credit or debit balances in a customer's account(s) may be offset by any other outstanding balance owed by or to the customer.

If offer card is missing write to: Silhouette Reader Service, 3010 Walden Ave., P.O. Box 1867, Buffalo NY 14240-1867

NO POSTAGE
NECESSARY
IF MAILED
IN THE
UNITED STATES

BUSINESS REPLY MAIL

FIRST-CLASS MAIL   PERMIT NO. 717-003   BUFFALO, NY

POSTAGE WILL BE PAID BY ADDRESSEE

SILHOUETTE READER SERVICE
3010 WALDEN AVE
PO BOX 1867
BUFFALO NY 14240-9952

GET FREE BOOKS and a FREE GIFT WHEN YOU PLAY THE...

Lucky 7

SLOT MACHINE GAME!

Just scratch off the silver box with a coin. Then check below to see the gifts you get!

YES! I have scratched off the silver box. Please send me the 2 free Silhouette Special Edition® books and gift for which I qualify. I understand I am under no obligation to purchase any books, as explained on the back of this card.

335 SDL DRRG   235 SDL DRRW

FIRST NAME	LAST NAME

ADDRESS

APT.#	CITY

STATE/PROV.	ZIP/POSTAL CODE

7	7	7	**Worth TWO FREE BOOKS plus a BONUS Mystery Gift!**
🍒	🍒	🍒	**Worth TWO FREE BOOKS!**
♣	♣	♣	**Worth ONE FREE BOOK!**
🔔	🔔	🍒	**TRY AGAIN!**

Visit us online at www.eHarlequin.com

(S-SE-01/03)

Offer limited to one per household and not valid to current Silhouette Special Edition® subscribers. All orders subject to approval.

© 2000 HARLEQUIN ENTERPRISES LTD. ® and TM are trademarks owned by Harlequin Books S.A. used under license.

DETACH AND MAIL CARD TODAY!

"One...*ten*." Turning on his heel, he strode away, heading toward Winnie's hangar. He didn't want to calm down. He wanted her to know exactly how mad he was.

By the time he got to her hangar she'd climbed out of the plane and was leaning against the tail, pushing the black machine into the small metal building tail first. He crossed his arms and waited on the blacktop for her to finish.

It didn't take her long. As soon as the plane was in, she strode out of the hangar, tossed him a black scowl and pulled the sliding door shut with a jerk.

He fixed her with a nasty scowl of his own and jabbed a finger toward the runway. "What the hell was that all about? Were you trying to kill yourself? Or just get even with me?"

She looked at him wide-eyed and innocent, her expression saccharin sweet as she batted her lashes at him Southern-belle–style. "What on earth could I possibly have to get even with you about?"

"Don't play games with me, Winnie. I'm as angry as you are right now. I know you think I pulled a fast one at the cabin. I know you think I was trying to seduce you to elicit information. But that kiss wasn't about anything but you and me."

Nothing but anger flashed in her eyes now. "That kiss couldn't have been about you and me, *Rand Michaels*. I didn't even know who *you* were."

She strode away from him, heading for the small

building that housed the airport's lobby and maintenance area, her stride long and angry.

He stalked after her, staying easily at her side. "You might not have known my real name, but it was the only thing missing from that kiss. The want was real, the need was real, the heat crackling between us sure as hell was real."

"Oh, please. How stupid do you think I am? The jig is up." She shook her head in disgust. "What is it about men that they have to come at everything in a backhanded, devious manner? If your CIA buddies wanted to know if I helped Tucker, why didn't they just come to my front door and say, 'We suspect you of aiding and abetting your spouse in the theft of fifty million dollars'? I would have been happy to tell them I didn't have anything to do with Tucker's little escapade. More than happy to tell them the jerk ran off with another sweetie. If they wanted his accomplice maybe they should be looking for *her*. But did they do that? No-o-o."

She jerked the lobby door open and strode into the building. "They brought you in, instead. Mr. Pretty-Boy, Woman-Magnet Smith. Figured they'd stick someone as handsome and sexy as you in the plane with me and boy I'd just start telling you my life story. And if I don't start talking, hey, no problem, you'll just seduce me. You'll get me to talk that way, right?" Disgust twisted her lips. "What a bunch of sleazeballs."

He looked around the building, glad to find it

empty. Cash and Talon must have already headed out. Thank God. The last thing he needed them to hear was Winnie calling him a pretty boy, woman magnet, for crying out loud. He'd never live it down. He quickly twisted the lock on the door to make sure they retained their privacy, and did his best to ignore her ugly accusation. He would let her run out of steam. And then it would be his turn.

She waved her hands angrily. ''What is so hard about using the truth that the entire male population shrinks away from it as if it were the antithesis of…I don't know, male pride or something.''

Forget about letting her wind down. After what she'd just put him through, he was in no mood to listen to a male-bashing lecture. ''Look,'' he broke in. ''I'm sorry the CIA chose the method they did to investigate you. But at the time they didn't know you were innocent.''

She tossed her hands in the air. ''They didn't know I was guilty, either.''

''No they didn't. But when a crime is committed, and there's an accomplice involved, seven times out of ten you can look to the nearest and dearest for your list of suspects. And believe it or not, the direct approach isn't the most effective when it comes to fighting the bad guys. It might be the most honorable, but it's generally the least proficient and it's quite often the most bloody. So if the CIA chooses other, better, safer methods, even though they sometimes bruise the sensibilities of the innocent caught in the case, you'll have to excuse them."

She snorted her outrage. "I do *not* have to excuse them for messing in my life. And what was Tucker's excuse for behaving like such a snake in the end? He managed to find the gall to tell me he was leaving. Why didn't he, while he was packing his things and saying goodbye, just say, 'Honey, not only am I leaving you, but I'm about to steal fifty million dollars from Uncle Sam and some big bad drug lord in South America? You might want to be on the look-out because when the CIA can't find me after the mission, they're probably going to come knocking at your door. And I don't plan to stick around for the arrests, either, so if the good guys miss rounding up some of bad guys, they'll probably be knocking at your door, too.'"

She shot him a hard, accusatory glance. "But I'll bet when Nieto's men knock on my door, they'll be more direct, won't they? No beating around the bush there. Thumbscrews and pretty, sharp little knives, right? *Right?*"

His gut clenched at the picture, but he couldn't deny its accuracy. "Yes."

She hissed in disdain. "Kind of ironic, isn't it, that the bad guys are the most honest men in this picture."

It wasn't ironic to him. To him it was just an old tired fact. "Welcome to the trenches, sweetheart. As for dear ol' Tuck, you had to know something was wrong with that marriage before he left you. From what little you've told me, it's clear you quit getting whatever you needed out of that marriage a long time ago. If you ever did. So why didn't you get out? Why did you wait around for him to finally pull the plug?''

She waved her hands angrily again. ''Well, forgive me. I thought he loved me. I thought we were going to have a beautiful life together some day. *I thought* I could make him happy.'' Anger vibrated in her voice, but pain shone in her eyes.

Guilt slashed at him again, but he didn't let up. He wasn't ever going to watch her scream over the pavement upside down in that damned plane again. ''Well, here's a news flash for you. It wasn't your job to make him happy any more than it was your responsibility to make your dad happy so he'd stay home. If you want to quit being victimized, quit being a victim. Quit trying to make everyone around you happy, for crying out loud. And quit waiting for someone to make you happy. Find out what *you* want in life, what makes *you* happy and then go out and get it.''

Tears of anger and pain sparkled in her eyes; her chin quivered. But defiance didn't let her break down and cry. She tipped that chin up and locked her gaze mutinously on his. ''Good advice, Michaels. And what I want right now, is you...*gone*. So make your calls and pack your bags and get.''

She jabbed a finger at the door he'd locked just minutes before.

He crossed his arms over his chest. "Unfortunately, that's not going to happen. While you might think you don't know anything about Tucker's whereabouts, you probably do. I have a whole battery of questions I need to ask. And then there's the little detail of Nieto and his men. Until they're caught you're going to need protection."

"Well, I certainly don't need it from you." She spun away from him and strode over to the pile of survival gear they'd used after the crash. Apparently, Cash and Talon had brought it in. She rummaged impatiently through the gear. She moved a few things out of her way and then pulled out the FAA required rifle, her eyes gleaming with steely satisfaction.

Great. What did she think she was going to do with that? Protect herself? Criminy. She'd already told him she didn't know how to use the thing. So now that she was mad she figured what? That she'd become Rambo. Or maybe her intent was simply to shoot him.

Double great.

She turned to him, green eyes crackling with fire. "You're absolutely right, it's not my responsibility to make anyone happy. Or to do anyone's job for them, either. You want Tucker. You go out and find him. Without my help. I want you and your twisted little friends out of my life. As for Nieto's men—"

she held the rifle up, a cold, humorless smile turning her lips "—bring 'em on. I'm in the mood for a little bloodletting." Without another word she strode by him, gave the door's lock a vicious twist and pushed outside.

Rand watched her go, frustration clawing at his hide. Could this mess possibly get any better? He stepped over to the survival gear and peeked inside the giant green duffle. The teeniest, tiniest—and probably the only bit of relief he was going to get in this mess—slid through him. Shaking his head, he reached in and pulled out the most important part of the rifle Winnie had just carried out. The ammunition.

Tossing the box in the air, he gave his head a fatalistic shake. At least when he showed up at her cabin against her wishes, she couldn't shoot him.

Chapter Eleven

Winnie stretched, reaching toward the low bed-room ceiling of her rented cabin. It was good to be home, but it had been a long, exhausting night of raging and crying and soul searching. Her eyes were red-rimmed and swollen, her face puffy and blotchy, her mind a scramble of questions and uncertainties.

Did she have a victim mentality? Had Tucker used her during their marriage because she'd let him? And her father? Had she let him use her, too?

She shook her head as the questions whirled around her. What was so wrong about being nice to people? Trying to make them happy? Weren't chil-dren *supposed* to want to please their parents?

Wasn't one spouse *supposed* to try to make the other one happy? Wasn't *that* what marriage was about?

Of course, as she'd looked back over her marriage last night she'd realized Tucker hadn't tried very hard to make *her* happy. Most of the compromising had been on her side. She sighed in frustration. So, maybe she *had* been a little overzealous about making their marriage work. Maybe she'd even been a little stupid. But a willing victim? She wasn't ready to concede that. And even if she *had* been, did that make *him* blameless?

She shook her head. She'd tangled with those thoughts and a million others just like them all night long. She needed a strong cup of coffee before she could face them this morning. She headed for the kitchen part of her living room/kitchen combo, looking out the big picture window in the living room as she went.

The sun was just peeking over the horizon, the soft light just beginning to bring the world into focus. Movement on the other side of the drive caught her attention. She froze, fear streaking through her. Nieto's men?

She half ducked, peering harder through the weak morning light. On closer inspection she recognized the form immediately. Gritting her teeth, she strode to the door and jerked it open. "*What* are you doing here, Michaels?"

A wicked-looking rifle slung across his back, the man was crouched next to a small tent, pounding one of the tent's stakes into the ground. He looked up, lifting a sardonic brow. "Planting a flower garden?"

"Very funny."

He shrugged. "Best I can do this morning. I had a long night. It's damned cold out here."

Outrage poured over her. He'd sat outside her cabin all night? After she'd told him to get lost? She hoped he'd frozen his butt off. "I thought I told you and your friends to go home."

"So you did." Turning his back on her, he returned to his stake, the sound of rock striking metal disturbing the peace of her little spot on earth.

Grimacing, she drew a breath to tell him to get in his car and leave, but a quick glance around told her it wasn't going to be that easy. "How did you get here? Where's your car?"

"I came with the unit Griff sent out to guard your cabin."

Her eyes popped wide. *"Unit?"*

He nodded. "Eight of us. The area around your cabin has been broken into quadrants. There's a man in each quadrant and a rover who will travel back and forth between them, carrying messages, making sure everyone's alert, etcetera. I'll be here. And Cash and Talon have set up a post about a half mile down your road. The Jeep's with them."

Oh, man. A whole troop of them. Well, she didn't care if there was an entire nation of them. They weren't invading her life any more than they already had. "Stop pounding that post in. I told you yesterday I wanted you gone. I mean it. And that includes your friends, too.''

He just shrugged and moved to the next stake. ''And I told you I wasn't going anywhere until this investigation is finished. Until Nieto's men are safely behind bars.''

''I don't *need* your protection. I have the rifle, remember?''

He came out of his crouch in that powerful, fluid way of his—like a panther gathering himself to spring on his prey. But he didn't pounce. He just stood there, the strap to his rifle making a distinct statement as it slashed across his chest. His brown-eyed gaze locked hard on to hers. ''Yeah, I remember. Go get it.''

She refused to be intimidated. ''Why? So you can take it away from me?''

His eyes narrowed to thin, warning slits. ''Just go get it.''

She wanted to refuse, but the edge to his tone coupled with that look hinted he might well get it himself if she didn't. So she quickly went into her bedroom, grabbed it from its resting place by the bed and hurried back to the front door. ''Here it is, but I'm not giving it to you.''

''I didn't ask you to.'' He pointed to a giant pine a good twenty feet to his left. ''Aim it at that tree and fire it.''

She shot him a snide look. ''What? You don't think I can hit anything with it?'' Of course, there was always the possibility that she couldn't. She

didn't know anything about guns. But since the
FAA's goal for having the rifle in the survival gear
was that anyone, knowledgeable or unknowledge-
able, could get food, how hard could it be? She was
pretty sure all she'd have to do was point the thing
and pull the trigger.

"Just do it." There was that hard, edgy tone
again.

Fine. If it would get him out of her drive, she'd
shoot the poor, innocent tree. She turned toward the
pine, her nerves jangling just enough to make her
palms sweat now that the moment to actually use
the weapon was upon her. But she took a steady
stance, one foot forward, one back, ignored the
slight trembling of her body and brought the rifle to
her shoulder.

The sites were right there, easy to find. She
looked down the middle of them to a spot in the
center of the tree's wide trunk. Holding her breath,
she pulled the trigger.

Click.

She started in surprise. Click? Not bang? She
looked at the rifle in her hands and then to Michaels.

He was shaking his head. "That's what I thought.
You don't have a clue what the hell you're doing
with that thing. You walked out of that hangar last
night with an empty weapon and no ammunition,
thinking you were ready to take on some bad guys
who actually *load* their weapons before they go
hunting for innocent victims."

A little shiver ran through her as she realized how

unprotected she'd been last night. Well, not completely unprotected. Rand had been right outside her cabin. And the rest of the little army was down the road and strewn throughout the woods. But if it hadn't been for them... A grudging wisp of gratitude threaded through her.

But one night of baby-sitting didn't earn Michaels forgiveness. Thinking about that kiss still made her feel used, embarrassed...stupid. And mad. And every time she saw him she thought about it. She wanted him and his friends gone. She squared her shoulders. "So I'll get some ammo."

He shook his head. "Oh, no you won't. A weapon in the hands of a rank amateur is a dangerous thing." He turned his back on her and pounded the last stake in as if the discussion was closed.

She ground her teeth. "I'll take a quick course. I'll be a pro in no time. And you don't have anything to say about it. I don't answer to you."

Stakes in, he started pulling the snap-up tent into position, completely ignoring her.

She stomped her foot. *"Take that tent down, dammit."*

He turned to her, his expression hard and uncompromising. "You need more than a weekend course in gun handling to go up against men like Nieto's soldiers. The tent stays. And so do I."

She scowled at him. "If I don't see that tent coming down in the next five seconds, I'm calling the sheriff. He's a friend of mine. I'm sure I can get him to escort you to the local jail on trespassing charges."

He just shrugged. "I'm not trespassing. The property you're renting stops on your side of the drive. This is public property over here. And I already stopped in and had a chat with the sheriff. Explained the situation to him. How dangerous Nieto's men are. He said it was fine if I camped here. No problem."

She narrowed her eyes on him. "Did you tell him I didn't want you here?"

"Yep. Explained you might be a little reluctant about the guard dog routine. But like you said, he's your friend, he likes you. He made it clear I wasn't to worry about your protests. Said if you wanted to holler at someone you should give him a call. He'd be happy to listen."

"But not remove you."

"Nope."

She clenched her hands in frustration.

"You want to get rid of me, Winnie, you're going to have to *help* us find Tucker. And the money. Once both are safely within Uncle Sam's clutches, Nieto's men won't have any reason to come after you."

Damn Tucker for dragging her into this mess. And damn Michaels for being a betraying jackal instead of the nice, honorable man she'd thought him to be. But if she wanted her life back, it looked as if she'd have to deal with him. But she didn't have to do it graciously. "Fine. I'll answer your questions. *After* I have a nice cup of hot coffee. Until then, you can sit out here and freeze."

Rand sat on the edge of Winnie's porch waiting for her to come join him. Her cabin was small with a wooden porch, one step off the ground, running the entire length. A split-log railing ran around the edges, leaving a narrow entranceway in front of the door. It was a simple abode. Cozy. Inviting. And it was tucked into what had to be one of the world's most beautiful spots.

Her small yard, filled with her blooming wild-flowers, gracefully gave way to birches and pines as it flowed away from the cabin. Behind the trees the Wrangell mountain range jutted majestically toward the blue sky with its barren rock and snowcapped peaks. Gorgeous. If a little chilly.

He rubbed at his arms, trying to create a little warmth. He hadn't packed heavy enough clothing for the climate here. His flannel shirt and fleece pull-over weren't enough. It would be nice if Winnie would take pity on him and bring him a cup of hot coffee when she came out to answer his questions, but he was pretty sure he shouldn't hold his breath. He'd already been kicking his heels for an hour. She'd probably finished the pot long ago.

Finally her door opened and she strode out, a big mug of steaming coffee in hand. A little ray of hope ran through him. But she sipped from the mug as she moved to the old weathered rocker sitting next to the door and sat.

A silent sigh of regret echoed through his head. Coffee would have to wait until he took the time to make his own fire.

Brows knit together unhappily, she turned her gaze on him. "So start asking your questions, Michaels. The sooner I get you off my porch and those soldiers out of my woods the happier I'll be."

The coffee sure hadn't improved her mood. But then she had every right to be angry and short with everyone involved in this fiasco. The best thing he could do for her was make this questioning as quick and painless as possible. And then find Tucker and the damned money so she could have her life back.

He swung around so he could see her, putting his back against one post framing the way to the door and resting his feet on the opposite one. "Okay, let's go back six months and move forward from there."

"Well, that makes life easy. I didn't see Tucker in the past six months." Her lip curled in contempt. "With the exception of the day he came home to pack and tell me he was leaving, of course."

That didn't make sense. "You're sure? You didn't see him at all during that time period?"

She shot him an annoyed look. "What? You think my husband comes home for a few days and I don't *notice* him?"

"Of course not," he soothed. "But six months is a fairly long time frame. Let's break it down, okay? Take it in steps."

"Fine."

"According to the courthouse papers the CIA

pulled, you filed for divorce just a few days before Tucker and I went to Colombia to start the sting. It makes sense you wouldn't have seen him after that point because once we were in South America we were too busy to leave. But the two months before that we were here in the States doing all the prep work that goes into an operation like that. There were days, weeks even during that time when he could have come home." He paused, giving her a chance to remember.

She just shot him a hard stare over the top of her mug. "The *only* day I saw him during that time period was the day he came home to tell me he was leaving. Which was about two weeks before I filed for the divorce."

"Okay. Go back a little further. I checked with the CIA. His calendar was clear for quite some time before we started the prep work on the Colombian sting. You sure you didn't see him then?"

"I told you, I didn't see him. He told me he was on a mission." Tears glistened in her eyes and she looked away, her anger giving way to hurt. "My guess is, he was shacked up with his new sweetie somewhere."

He wanted to take her in his arms. Hold her. Comfort her. God help him, kiss her. Which was a damned foolish want. She sure as hell wouldn't appreciate it. He sure as hell shouldn't be *thinking* about doing it. He sighed. "Sorry."

She swiped at the tears. "Just ask your questions, Michaels."

He shifted his focus back on the case. "Okay, what about phone calls? Surely he called you during that period."

"A couple of times, yeah. But he didn't tell me where he was or what he was doing. I told you, he never shared anything related to his job. He just mouthed the usual platitudes. He was all right and he'd be home...whenever." Pain flashed on her face again.

He steeled himself against the need to comfort her and pushed on. "What about background noises?"

She shrugged. "He was in a bar. He's *always* in a bar when he calls. So there's lots of noise, lots of music, but nothing distinguishable, believe me."

"Actually, there's quite a bit about noise that's distinguishable if you know what you're listening for. For instance, did you hear voices in the background?"

"Probably, but—"

"Think," he coaxed, hoping he could get her to remember *something*. "If you heard voices, you heard a language. Were they speaking English or something foreign?"

Irritation twisted her lips, but she closed her eyes and thought. Finally, she shook her head. "Sorry, if I heard a foreign language, I didn't notice."

"What about the music? Rock or something more colloquial?"

"Michaels," she snapped, irritation getting the best of her. "I said, nothing distinguishable. I meant nothing distinguishable. Can't the CIA look at my phone records and tell where he called from?''

He shook his head. ''The only thing phone records tell us is who you called. Calls made *to* you can't be traced.''

''Well, I'm sorry. But I can't help you, either. Noise might very well have its own little distinguishing sounds, but I wasn't listening for them. I had no idea my husband was about to dump me and run away with his own little Mata Hari and fifty million bucks.''

And he was quite certain being reminded she'd been dumped and having to go over it and over it wasn't much fun, so he checked his own frustration and moved on. ''Okay, what about the last time you saw Tucker? When he was packing his bags and saying goodbye? What did he tell you about the woman he was running off with?''

''Nothing beyond the fact she existed.''

''He didn't tell you her name?''

''No. And I asked. But he's not an idiot. He wasn't going to leave any clues behind for me to give the CIA or Nieto's men when they came knocking.''

''No, probably not. But I was hoping.'' He thought for a moment. ''We need to figure out why he came home that one last time.''

Hurt and anger flashed in her eyes. ''You don't think I deserved an in-person goodbye?''

He shot her a reproving glance. ''That's not what I said. I think you deserve a lot more than Tucker

ever gave you. You certainly deserved better than to
be left holding the bag. But considering he was willing to leave you holding the bag, and very possibly
facing some very nasty men, I find it hard to believe
he came home because he felt honor bound to say
goodbye in person.''

Tears glistened in her eyes as she realized even
Tucker's goodbye had been a betrayal.

Man, he hated this job. But the best thing he could
do for her was get it over with. Dig out any information she might unknowingly have in her head and
find Tucker and the money. That, at least, would get
Nieto off her tail. ''He came home for a reason,
Winnie. There must have been something at the
house he needed. You said he packed some things.
Do you remember what?''

She shook her head, doing her best to hide her
pain from him. ''He told me he was leaving practically the second he walked in the door, so I was
pretty stunned while he packed.''

''We'll take it slow then. He packed clothes?''

She heaved a frustrated sigh of her own and took
a sip of coffee. ''Yes.''

''What about bad-weather gear? Coats? Wind-
breakers?''

She shook her head. ''We keep those in the front
closet, and he didn't leave the bedroom while he
packed. In fact, the only two rooms he visited while
he was there were the living room, where he told
me he was leaving, and the bedroom. Then he was
gone.''

"Okay, that's good. That means whatever he came for was in one of those rooms."

She shook her head. "No, it had to have been in the bedroom. He didn't take anything from the living room, I'm positive."

"Okay. Did he keep anything besides clothes in the bedroom? Was there a desk? Maybe he took some papers?"

She shook her head. "The desk was in the den, and he didn't go in there. Besides, I was the only one who used it. I was the one at home. The one who paid the bills and kept track of the insurance policies and everything else that had paperwork attached to it. And before you ask, no, I didn't see any suspicious papers in the months before he left. Or any other time for that matter."

"All right. What about trinkets? Did he have a box in the bedroom where he kept trinkets? Jewelry. Keys. That kind of thing? Maybe he picked up a key to a safety deposit box?"

"Actually, we did share a jewelry box. And he did look in it." Her brows furrowed in concentration. "Rather carefully I might add. But he must have decided he could get much nicer things with his fifty mil because he didn't take anything."

"You're sure?"

"Positive. He just closed the box with an irritated huff, zipped his bag and waved goodbye."

Dead end.

Disappointment stabbed at him. He'd hoped for a clue that would lead them to Tucker so she'd be out of danger. He wanted her safe. But like everything else in this case, it wasn't going to be that easy.

"So? What do you think?"

He shrugged. "I think you'd best get used to me on your porch and soldiers in your woods. We're going to be here awhile."

Chapter Twelve

Later that afternoon Winnie stood in front of her bathroom mirror, twisting her hair on top of her head and securing it with an alligator clip. After the past twenty-four hours she felt as if a 747 had taxied over her. And she looked like it.

She'd tried to rest after Michaels had asked his questions this morning, to get rid of the dark circles under her eyes, but sleep had eluded her. She was sad and mad and little bit afraid.

Okay, a lot afraid.

The CIA. Drug lords. Fifty million missing dollars. Sounded like a crash-and-burn scenario to her, and she'd already scraped through one of those this week. She wasn't up for another.

She sighed. How could she possibly have lived with Tucker for the past four years and not known who he really was? Of course, she hadn't really lived with him for the past two years. He'd been gone far more than he'd been home. Far, far more.

She sighed again. Okay, her marriage *had* been in serious trouble for a while now. So why hadn't she realized it?

Or had she? A little voice niggled in the back of her head, whispering that she *had* worried about her marriage when Tucker's absences had gotten longer and longer. Reminding her that she *had* promised herself several times she'd confront him about it the next time he came home.

So why hadn't she?

Easy answer.

Because she'd wanted the dream so badly. And she'd been afraid if she confronted Tucker about their marriage, he'd leave. Just as her father had left a thousand times before. So she'd settled for what little time she and Tucker had together. And she'd settled for what little affection he was willing to offer on those short visits. Just so she could hold on to her dream—a home, a family, someone to love.

Someone to love her.

She stared at her reflection in the mirror. Unfortunately, pretending nothing was wrong hadn't saved her marriage. Or her dream. Maybe it *was* time she started thinking about making herself happy.

No maybe. It *was* time.

Today. Now. This instant.

New resolution. She was *never* going to beg for love again. This was her life. And she was going to live it. Not for a father who remembered her only when he needed money. Or for a husband who apparently never remembered her at all. But for herself.

She smiled wryly. Now, if she just knew how to go about it. And what it was she wanted.

Well, it might take her a while to get a complete master plan together, but step one was easy. Getting back to work. She needed to fly. Needed something that gave her peace. And that meant she had to keep the appointment Henry made for her at the doctor this afternoon. She glanced at her watch. Best get a move on.

She rushed out of the bathroom, grabbed her purse as she zipped through the living room and strode out of the house. Digging into her purse for the car keys, she headed for her car. And came to a stumbling halt.

That arrogant snake.

Anger simmering in her veins, she strode over to her little yellow Geo. "What are you doing in my car?"

Michaels looked up from where he'd made himself at home in the driver's seat. "Getting ready to take you to your doctor's appointment."

She sputtered in outrage. "How did you know I *had* a doctor's appointment?"

"I called Henry this morning. I promised to charter a plane from him to take you to Jenny's house, remember?''

She remembered.

''He said you weren't getting in any plane of his until you'd been to the doctor. And then he told me you had an appointment this afternoon. At one o'clock, right? We'd better get going because Henry asked me to have you at the airport by two-thirty. The FAA guys will be there.''

She stared at the rifle Michaels had stuck between the bucket seats, within easy reach if he needed it. She didn't know why that rifle looked so much deadlier than the one she'd taken from the survival gear. But it did. It definitely did. And she didn't want to get into the car with it. Or him.

She crossed her arms under her breasts. ''You are not my secretary, Michaels. Or my bodyguard. You want to sit on my porch and guard my house, have at it. But I am not dragging you around with me, so you might as well get out of the car.''

''You're right. I'm not your secretary. But I am absolutely your bodyguard, and you're not going *anywhere* without me. So *you* might as well get in the car.''

She grabbed hold of her temper. ''Look, if Nieto's men show up anywhere, it'll be here. Not at the doctor's office. Which means I'm not going to need you there, but your friends down the road might very well need you here.''

''You don't know where Nieto's men are going to show up and neither do I. As for my friends down the road, they can take care of themselves, trust me.''

She snorted at the comment. ''I think we both know how foolish that would be.''

He heaved a tired sigh. ''Are you going to get in the car or call the doctor and tell him you're not coming? If you're going to choose the latter, be sure to call Henry afterward and tell him you won't be flying tomorrow.''

Frustration poured through her. She was flying tomorrow. Come hell or high water. With an irritated huff she stormed around the car and got in the passenger's side, slamming the door behind her. ''This isn't fair and you know it.''

He shrugged, holding his hand out for her keys. ''I figured out life wasn't fair my first year at the Agency. Hope for something short of evisceration and total chaos. You'll be less disappointed that way.''

She slapped the keys into his palm. ''Now there's a cheery attitude.''

''Like I said, it was a long night.''

If it had been forty-below last night his night could not have been half as long as hers. But she didn't comment. She wasn't up to the verbal sparring. ''Do you know where you're going?''

He slid the keys into the ignition and turned the engine over. ''Toward town.''

And he seemed to know which direction that was, so she sat silently, watching the countryside go by and trying not to notice the tension in the car. But it was impossible. It grew thicker with every mile they covered.

When the highway appeared that led to her doctor's she pointed stiffly to it. "Turn right there."

Michaels turned onto the road and then glanced her way. "It occurs to me that this whole thing might go a little easier if we come to some sort of truce."

"Truces don't work without at least a hint of trust. And I think I've already made myself clear on that matter."

He stared out the windshield, his expression grim—and if she didn't know better, she'd say troubled. Finally he shot her a sideways glance. "Look, I'm not going to apologize for coming in undercover. I was doing my job, and that's how it's done. But I do apologize for kissing you. That I never should have done."

"Gee, ya think?" She packed as much sarcasm into her words as she could muster.

His lips pressed into a hard line. "I shouldn't have kissed you, but not for the reason you're thinking."

She raised an outraged brow. "So you think it's acceptable to seduce a woman for a job? A woman you know is innocent."

"On the whole, no, I don't. But I could probably come up with a scenario where I would find it acceptable. If I thought that was the only way to save lives, I'd do it. I haven't ever done it—just for the record—but I would if it was necessary. But I wasn't seducing you out there. That kiss had nothing to do with my job.''

She snorted in disbelief.

He took his gaze from the road and locked it on hers. ''It didn't. I kissed you for one reason and one reason only. I wanted to.'' The words had the same hard edge as the ones he'd used earlier when he'd told her to get the rifle.

But she wasn't buying it. ''Yeah, right.''

He looked back to the road. ''Listen, do you think you're the only person on earth who has longed for domestic bliss and had it blow up in your face? I longed for it once, too. Dreamed about having a family, a home and a sweet, loving woman. Until I realized I couldn't have any of it. That life will never be anything but a fantasy for me. But out in those woods…''

His gaze took on a faraway look. ''You were everything I'd dreamed of in a woman—pretty and smart and sweet…''

She huffed in disgust. ''You make me sound like Shirley Temple.''

A hint of a smile turned his lips. ''Not quite. Shirley Temple was pretty and smart and sweet in a cute little adorable way. Kinda like a cuddly puppy. You're pretty and smart and sweet in a sexy, hot, fully adult way. Nothing at all like a cuddly puppy.'' His voice got rougher with each word out of his mouth. And there was a matching intensity in his eyes that made her think he just might be telling the truth.

A traitorous heat slid through her. She wanted to believe him. Wanted to believe some of the good times they'd had in the woods had been real. That he'd enjoyed fishing with her and talking with her and laughing with her.

She wanted to believe all the passion she'd felt when he'd kissed her had been real.

But lying was his business. She wasn't going to be a pushover this time around. He was going to have to make her believe. "I find it hard to buy that a worldly-wise man like you would find someone as ordinary as me anything but…mildly amusing."

"Worldly wise?" He laughed humorlessly. "Is there such a thing? World weary perhaps. And I am that. But you, Winnie Mae Taylor, are anything but ordinary. And stuck in the woods with you…"

She shouldn't ask. Shouldn't push.

But she had to know. *Had* to know if that kiss, the most incredible kiss she'd ever experienced, was real. "Stuck in the woods with me, what?"

"Look, you were never supposed to find out who I really was. When the mission was over, we were both supposed to go our separate ways. And I thought, what harm could there be if I stole a few days for myself? If I enjoyed your company and pretended for just a little while that I was a normal guy stranded in the woods with a beautiful woman." He stared out the windshield, his expression bleak. "I just wanted to taste your sweetness. One kiss. That's all I wanted."

The longing in his words seemed so real.

The temptation to believe him pulled at her like a turbine engine sucking in air. She wanted to believe him. Wanted to believe that someone would feel that way about her. Wanted to believe that she might be someone's dream.

But did she?

Chapter Thirteen

Winnie sat in the pilot's seat of the Beech 18 thankful the doc had given her the okay to go back to work yesterday. She felt in control here. In a plane. In the sky. At least a little bit in control. Rand was in the right-hand seat. Proof that a good portion of her life was anything but in control. But the comforting growl of twin radial engines thrummed in her ears, and she was on her way to Anchorage to pick up cargo, her normal Thursday route. It might only be a bit of normalcy, but she was grateful for it.

It had been another sleepless night of soul searching. If that kiss had been real, if that electrifying moment of passion and heat had been real, what then?

Did she want to just file it away as a wonderful memory? A warm thought to spice up the quiet, independent life she had planned? Or, if that explosive, mind-blowing kiss was real, did she still *want* an independent life? That was the kind of kiss that could make a woman think very hard before excluding men from her life. At least one very specific man. Which brought her to another set of questions.

If that kiss was real, when this mission was over, did she want Michaels to disappear? Or did she want to ask him to stay, at least for a little while? Long enough for them to see if that passion could turn into something deeper?

Whoa. She was getting way ahead of herself. *Way* ahead. She wasn't even positive that kiss was real. Not yet. And she needed more information than she'd gotten yesterday to figure it out. He'd said something in the car the other day that, thinking back on it, she realized she'd ignored.

Today she wasn't going to ignore it.

She glanced at him from the corner of her eye. He was staring out the windshield, his rifle propped between his knee and the plane's door, his expression as pensive as she imagined her own to be.

As if sensing her perusal, he looked over at her. The corners of his mouth turned down just a hair. "I'm sorry about Jenny's birthday. I know you're not happy about putting it off." His apology crackled through the headset.

She shrugged. "It's okay. When this is over I'll get together with her. We'll do the birthday thing then.'' Just as he'd promised, he'd offered to charter her services from Henry today. Have her fly them out to Jenny's so she could spend the day with the new teen, celebrating the girl's birthday. But Winnie had declined.

The last report had Nieto's men still in the lower forty-eight, but they were heading this way. While she felt confident they couldn't chase her down if she was hopping from one stop to another, she wasn't so sure they couldn't find her if she flew to someone's house and stayed the day. She wasn't willing to take the risk she'd lead them straight to Jenny.

Michaels nodded. ''I'll rent one of Henry's planes for you to fly out there when you go. That way it won't cost you or Henry anything for the extra trip.''

She didn't need him to pay for the plane, but she had a feeling talking him out of it wouldn't be easy. And she had more important things she wanted to talk to him about. ''Fine. Talk to Henry. In the meantime, I have a question for you.''

Wariness pulled his brows low, but he nodded. ''Shoot.''

''Do you remember saying yesterday that you shouldn't have kissed me?''

His wariness increased. ''I remember.''

''Well, I want to know why you think you shouldn't have. You said it wasn't for the reason I thought. Which I assume means it doesn't have anything to do with the reprehensibleness of seducing a woman for your job.''

He shot her a slanted look. "I repeat, that kiss had nothing to do with the job."

"Yes, so you said. And I'm entertaining the thought of believing you. But I need more information. So if the job wasn't the reason you shouldn't have kissed me, what *was?*"

He shook his head. "Let it go, Winnie. It was a mistake. Rehashing it won't change that."

"Maybe not. But I want to rehash it. And you owe me. So cough it up, Super Spy. Why shouldn't you have kissed me?"

He shot her a hard stare, trying to intimidate her, get her to back down.

She stared right back. "Why not, Michaels?"

With a frustrated huff, he dug his fingers into his eyes. "There's no purpose to this."

"You don't get to be the judge of that. I do."

Exhaustion and reluctance merged on his face, but when he looked back to her, he met her gaze. "Look, you're a sweet, loving woman with a good, caring heart. And I...well, I'm exactly what you called me the other day. A sleazeball. A man like me doesn't belong anywhere near a woman like you."

Of all the things she'd expected to hear, that wasn't it. She cocked her head, studying him. "If that kiss wasn't about seducing me for the job, why are you a sleazeball?"

"I might be innocent on that one little charge, but I'm guilty as hell on a million others." He shook his head, remorse shadowing his expression. "A man doesn't spend as many years in covert operations as I have without the muck rubbing off on him.''

Her stomach clenched at the self-disdain she heard in his words. She wasn't naive enough to believe that the kind of work the CIA did—protecting the nation's security—was anything other than dangerous, dirty work. She'd always been amazed that working as an agent hadn't seemed to take a bigger toll on Tucker. But perhaps it had. Perhaps that's why he'd eventually crossed the line to the other side. But whatever effects it'd had on Tuck, it had obviously had a very different effect on this man. ''You think you're a sleazeball because of the things you've had to do for the job?''

''And you don't? Should I remind you of what you said about the backhanded, devious manner of men in general and CIA agents and mercenaries in particular?''

''I was mad then. I've cooled down now. Had some time to think things through a little more clearly. And as much as I hated being a pawn, I can understand why the case was handled the way it was. I'm not sure you can classify yourself as a sleazeball because you've had to do unsavory things for your job.''

He shook his head. ''You can say that because you don't know the names of the innocent people that have been sacrificed so the people of this country could lay their heads down at night and sleep in peace. I do.''

Oh, God. He was right. She couldn't possibly understand what it was like to do what he did. But looking at the downturn of his lips, the shadows in his eyes and feeling the unhappiness that seemed to emanate from him, she had to wonder if it wasn't long past time when he should have stopped doing it. "Maybe it's time you got out."

A cold, humorless laugh echoed through the headset. "Tried that once. Didn't stick."

"Why not?"

"Are you kidding? What do you think I have in common with the normal Joe or Jane? What do you think I would have to say to them? Do you think they want to hear how many people I killed last month? Last week? Do you think they'd understand *why* I had to kill them?"

"For pity's sake, you don't have to start your conversation with a body count."

"No, but once you tell someone you worked for the CIA, the conversation works its way around to that every time. And even if people could understand it, why on earth would I want to bring that kind of ugliness into anyone's life?"

"So don't tell people you worked for the CIA. Make up a past. You ought to be a pro at that by now."

A sad smile crossed his lips. "You think I didn't think of that? You think that wasn't my original plan? It was. I constructed a past, put all the paperwork in order, bought a place and tried to start a new life."

"And?"

"And it worked for a few months. I had a nice little house with a nice porch, great for sitting on and watching the sun set or drinking a cold one. I had good neighbors, a mundane but acceptable job. But after a while I realized it was an exercise in futility. I'd left the CIA because I was tired of the lies, tired of pretending to be someone I wasn't. And there I was, doing the same thing. Lying. Pretending."

"Of course it was rough in the beginning. The CIA was your entire past, so whenever you talked to anyone about anything you had to lie. But time would ease that problem. Eventually you would have a real past to talk about."

He shrugged. "Maybe it would have gotten easier. But in the end it still would have been a life built on a lie. Which is a tolerable existence, I suppose, for a man living on his own. But I didn't want a solitary life. I wanted that dream, remember? The home. The wife. A dozen little rug rats."

Her jaw dropped. "A dozen?"

He chuckled softly. "I would have settled for less, but it was a moot point. There wasn't ever going to be a Mrs. Rand Michaels."

She had a hard time believing that. She'd been kissed by the man. "Why on earth not? The neighbors were comfortable with you. There's no reason a woman wouldn't have been just as comfortable."

His brows shot toward his hairline and he looked at her as if she'd completely skipped Life 101. "You can't lie to a woman you plan to marry about who you really are. You can't build a marriage on lies and half truths. You of all people should know that.''

Okay, she should know that. She did know that. And if she needed proof all she had to do was look at her own failed marriage. Tucker had been lying to her for a long time, or at the very least he hadn't been telling her the whole truth. He'd kept secrets from her. Secrets about his job. Secrets about himself. With or without his leaving, her marriage would have eventually crumbled. Because she'd wanted more. And she wanted to think that sooner or later she would have demanded it.

''You're right, a marriage based on lies doesn't work. Sooner or later it falls apart. But you wouldn't have had to lie to her forever. Once you'd found the right woman, you could have told her the truth. If she loved you, your past wouldn't have mattered to her.''

''What dream world are you living in? All I did was *kiss* you, and when you found out I was Rand Michaels instead of Bob Smith you wanted to wring my neck. And you had every right to.''

''I didn't say she wouldn't want to scalp you after she found out. But if she loved you, really loved you, she'd get over it. And then you could have your real marriage.''

He shook his head. ''You're missing the point. Lies aside, I didn't want to bring the ugliness of my past into my neighbors' lives, what on earth makes you think I'd want to bring it into the life of the woman I loved? So I went back to work. But in the private sector this time. I could pick my jobs that way. Do my best to stay away from the really nasty cases.''

She stared at him, words failing her. She didn't know if his decision had been selfless and wise—or cowardly and unutterably stupid. But she did know...

That kiss had been real.

A man who'd denied himself the very life he dreamed of to spare his neighbors and the abstract woman of his dreams the unpleasantness of his past wouldn't seduce a woman for a job. Not unless he had to. And no lives had been on the line in those woods.

That kiss—that mind-numbing, flesh-tingling kiss—had been real.

Chapter Fourteen

The next morning Winnie stared out the plane's windshield. It was Friday. Delivery day. The back of the plane was filled with mail, some of the packages she'd picked up yesterday and a few groceries and provisions she'd picked up last evening after they'd returned from Anchorage. Things people who didn't get to town often needed.

She and Rand were in the Cessna 185 this morning. Smaller, quieter, slower, but it handled the grass runways with joie de vivre and sneaked into tight spots with the ease of a cat burglar. A definite plus out here in the bush.

The sky was clear with just enough small, puffy clouds to make it cheery. A perfect match for her mood. She'd finally managed to get some sleep last night, and she felt a whole lot better for it. There were still a million questions in her head. About her life. About Rand Michaels. But she wasn't going to think about any of them today.

She needed a day to relax. Regroup. The last week had been one roller-coaster ride after another. She didn't want to think about making life-altering decisions today. A day or two of thinking about something else, letting her current problems mull over in the back of her head, would undoubtedly give her a clearer perspective on things. So today she was going to enjoy herself.

And so far she was having a bang-up time. It was good to see the people she delivered mail to. She'd missed them. Good to catch up on what they'd been doing over the past week. And they'd been as excited to see her as she had been to see them. Whether their communication system was computer, radio or the ever-present ham radio, they'd all known when she'd gone missing and when she'd been found.

As a result, they'd all rushed out to greet her, their faces filled with worry until she'd stepped out of the plane and they'd seen for themselves that she was all right. Then they'd swept her into their arms for giant hugs before ushering her and Rand into their houses so she could tell them her tale of the crash over cookies and ice cream. It had been a novel experience for her. A wonderful experience. She'd never felt a part of a community before. Hadn't realized until this morning how much of this community she'd become.

And Rand's company seemed to make everything that much more special. With the controversy of the kiss behind them, the comradery they'd had in the woods had returned.

So had the sexual tension.

They were both ignoring it. A good decision—for today. But a little voice in the back of her head warned that she'd be sorry, really sorry, if she let Rand walk out of her life without at least exploring what might be between them. But she wasn't going to complicate today with it.

She looked down at the wild terrain below and pointed to a cabin in the distance. "That's our next stop. Mary Long's place. You're gonna like her. She's a fly fisherman."

He smiled. "Yeah? I like Mary already."

He'd seemed to like everyone he'd met this morning. And everyone had liked him. He might think he didn't belong in normal society, but she thought he would fit perfectly here. The wildness of Alaska seemed like a good home for a panther. The people here weren't faint at heart. They could handle his past. Of course, convincing Rand of that might not be so easy.

Forcing her thoughts back to the moment, she lined up with the short stretch of mown grass in front of Mary's cabin and started to push the plane downward. "Steady the cake, will you Rand, while I put this thing down."

The Cooper kids had made a chocolate cake for her safe return. The pictures they'd drawn on the top with colored icing were indecipherable, but it was a colorful creation and despite the abstract art it looked yummy. And the fact that the tots had made it especially for her would make it taste even better.

Reaching back, Rand steadied the cake as she hit the ground and bounced over the rough terrain toward the cabin. Mary was already rushing out of her cabin and heading their way as Winnie brought the plane to a halt.

Mary's gray ponytail bounced on her back as she traveled quickly over the rough ground, her well-worn hat with its wide brim and multitude of brightly colored fishing flies shading her eyes. Winnie had always been amazed at how quickly Mary moved. For a woman in her late sixties she was in great shape.

As soon as they crawled out of the plane, Mary grabbed Winnie's shoulders, her sharp eyes raking her from head to toe. "You look all right. Any hidden injuries?"

Winnie smiled. She'd purposefully worn a long-sleeved shirt to avoid any questions or worries over her arm. But, as usual, Mary was one step ahead of her.

Winnie chuckled and shook her head. "I got a small cut on my arm in the crash. But, it's nothing. I'm fine, Mary."

Mary turned that sharp gaze to Rand. "You the man with her when the plane went down?"

"Yes, ma'am," Rand answered, his eyes twinkling.

"Is the cut as small and insignificant as she says?"

He smiled. "No, ma'am. But it's healing well."

The older woman grunted and turned back to Winnie. "Are you taking care of it?"

Winnie rolled her eyes. "Yes, Mary, I am. And before you spend the next half hour grilling me about it, let's change the subject. Did you know Rand was a fly fisherman?" That was a subject Mary couldn't ignore.

Mary's sharp gaze swung to Rand, interest replacing the worry. "Is that right?"

Rand shot Winnie a knowing glance, but the smile on his lips was genuine as he answered Mary. "Yes, ma'am. I love the sport."

"You come to Alaska to fish?" Hope flashed in Mary's eyes.

He tipped a shoulder. "Partly."

"Had any luck?"

Winnie winced, his fishing luck had definitely taken a downturn when he'd stepped into her life. "His rod burned with the plane—before he had a chance to use it."

Mary frowned. "Now there's some bad luck. What kind of rod was it? Nothing fancy, I hope."

Winnie groaned. Maybe this hadn't been the best subject to bring up. "It was very fancy. A Thomas and Thomas, passed down from his grandfather."

Real pain crossed the woman's face. "A Thomas

and Thomas classic. Now there's some bad news. Could never afford one myself. But I've used one a few times.'' She smiled fondly, remembering. ''There's just something special about those rods. A grace. A mystique almost. Know what I mean?''

An answering fondness filled Rand's gaze. ''Yes, ma'am. I know exactly what you mean.''

Winnie's heart squeezed. The rod might be gone, but it was obvious the memories around it were still there. She was glad for that.

Mary nodded. ''Well you're young. With any luck, you'll have time to replace it. Meanwhile, I got an extra rod you can borrow while you're here. Nothing as fine as a Thomas and Thomas, but it'll do the trick.''

Not for the first time today, Winnie was reminded of how generous the people here were. Mary didn't know Rand from Adam, and yet, she was willing to loan him one of her possessions.

Rand shook his head. ''Thank you. But I'm afraid there won't be time to fish. I've got some business to take care of, and then I've got to rush back.''

''Too bad. No place like Alaska for fishing,'' Mary said. ''Maybe next time around.''

He looked around him with that expression of longing he always got when he looked at the countryside. ''Maybe.''

But Winnie knew there wouldn't be another time around. If he left, it would be for good.

Shaking off the sense of emptiness that that thought brought, she reached into the plane and grabbed Mary's mail and the package she'd picked up at the pharmacy. She turned back to Mary, extending the hand with the envelopes. "Mail."

Mary quickly shuffled through the short stack. "All junk."

Now Winnie held the box out to the older woman. "Insulin—and a message from the doc."

Mary's faced scrunched in distaste. "What does that old coot want?"

Winnie put on her sternest face. "Says he needs you to come in for a checkup, Mary, before he renews your prescription."

The woman snorted. "Tell him to take a hike."

Winnie huffed in exasperation. "Come on, he's concerned about you. Says it's been two years since you've been in. He's worried you're not getting the right amount of insulin."

"Worried. Schmorried. That old man just likes to stick needles in people."

Winnie laughed. "Maybe. God knows he stuck enough in me the other day, taking blood, giving me a tetanus booster. But he's not going to send more insulin with me until you go in. So go in already."

Mary's lips turned down and she looked away. "It's a long drive. My eyes aren't what they used to be."

Winnie suddenly realized she was worried about making the drive into town. And too proud to ask someone to drive her. She shrugged. "So I'll fly you. Two weeks from today. Put it on your calendar. I'll tell the doc you're coming."

The woman grimaced. ''You have better things to do with your time than—''

''Oh, stop it. It's my time. I want to fly you to town with it, I will.''

Mary huffed, but she nodded. ''Fine. Tell the quack I'm coming. Now, come inside while I make your friend a sandwich. Yours is already made.'' She headed back to her cabin, her pace as quick as it had been earlier.

Winnie scrambled after her. ''Mary, don't go to any trouble. Really, he can share mine.'' That way they'd have only one sandwich to toss out when they got back to Henry's.

''Don't be silly. He's a big strapping boy. He needs his own food. Won't take me but a minute. And then you can be on your way.''

Winnie knew a losing battle when she heard one. ''Okeydokey then.''

While Mary made the sandwich, she and Rand waited in the living room. She dropped into a chair, but Rand walked over to the big picture window and stared out. He was admiring the countryside again. She was pretty sure he was going to miss it when he left. She wondered if he'd miss her. Again the disquieting feeling that she would miss him—quite a bit—assailed her.

Mary strode out of the kitchen, carrying two sandwiches wrapped in wax paper. She handed them to Rand. ''If you find more time on your hands than you thought, you come back. We'll do some fishing.''

"You got it." He shook the woman's hand, and then they were on their way back to the plane.

Winnie had the plane in the air two minutes later. She turned to Rand, chuckling. "She's a character, isn't she?"

"That she is. But you were right, I like her."

"Yeah, I do, too. As a matter of fact I like all of this." The realization came out of the blue, but there was nothing shaky or iffy about it. It was clear and strong and true. Apparently, letting things mull over in the back of her head was amazingly effective.

He raised a brow. "All of this?"

"Yeah. All of this." She waved her hand, encompassing the plane and its contents. "I like living in my little cabin and working for Henry and flying the mail."

She stared out the windshield, joy and a sense of rightness sliding through her. "You know, I realized the other morning you were right. I have spent a good portion of my life trying to make others happy. So I'm taking charge of my life. I'm figuring out what *I* want."

She paused for a minute, smiling as excitement skittered through her. "I first came to Alaska because aviation jobs are easy to find here, and I needed a job. Fast. The job Henry offered me wasn't overly lucrative, but it started right away and I figured it would do until I found a fancier job. One where I'd be flying bigger planes. Making more money so I could pay those bills off faster. You know what I mean?"

He nodded. "Most people keep their eyes open for a better position."

"Well, not me. Not anymore. I don't want a better job. I want this one. I like it here. I like flying the mail. I like these people. I like looking after them." She just couldn't stop smiling as the decision solidified in her mind. "I like the way they look after me."

Rand returned her smile full force. "Good for you."

She tapped a happy jig on the yoke with her fingers. "Yeah. Good for me."

He unwrapped one of Mary's sandwiches and handed it to her. "I think this deserves a celebration."

She set the sandwich in her lap, laughing. "Oh, no, we definitely don't want to celebrate with these. In fact, we don't want to eat these at all."

"Speak for yourself. I'm hungry. Cookies and ice cream are nice, but I want real food." He lifted the sandwich toward his mouth.

"Rand, don't." She tried to swipe the sandwich from his hands.

He easily avoided her attempt and took a giant bite.

Revulsion rippled through her. "Ewww."

To her amazement he chewed, swallowed and shrugged without so much as the slightest gag. "What? It's fine."

She stared at him in horror. "It's liver and anchovies and grape *jam.*'' A hard shiver ran through her just thinking about it.

He shrugged. ''Sounds nutritious. Lots of protein. And a little bit of sugar for quick energy.'' He took another bite.

She closed her eyes tight, trying to block the sight. ''Oh, God, stop it already. What's wrong with you? Don't you have any taste buds?''

''Of course I do. But I learned to quit tasting things with them a long time ago.''

She snapped her eyes open at that comment. ''That's not possible.''

He took another bite and chuckled at the face she made. ''Of course it is. It's a trick. Like teaching yourself not to feel pain. Spook school—Tricks To Keep from Tipping Off Your Enemies.''

She narrowed her eyes on him. Was he telling the truth or teasing her?

He held his hand up, laughing. ''It's true, I swear.''

''What does learning not to taste something have to do with not tipping your enemies off?''

''Are you kidding? Do you have any idea the kind of places I usually get sent to do my job?''

''Considering the way you look at these mountains, I'm guessing most of them aren't this nice.''

He shook his head. ''Not even close. My usual destination is some third-world hell hole. Do you know what they eat in places like that?''

She shook her head. If it made eating liver, anchovy and jam sandwiches acceptable she maybe didn't want to know.

"Try snakes, bugs...*monkeys,* for crying out loud. Have you ever *seen* a monkey boiling in a pot?" He grimaced. "It looks like a little baby. Arms, legs, head. God, it's awful."

She shuddered. "You didn't eat it, did you?"

"You bet I did. I've eaten all those things. If I'm undercover I'm usually trying to convince the people I'm one of them. And if I'm one of them, eating bugs and monkey should be natural to me. That's where not tipping off your enemy comes in. I don't eat the monkey, they figure out I'm not who I say I am."

She shuddered again. "Okay, I get it. But you're not in one of those horrible places now. So there's no reason why you have to eat that awful sandwich."

He shrugged. "Except I'm hungry and it's filling. And after all these years, it doesn't matter what I eat."

"What do you mean it doesn't matter? You might know how to turn them off, but your taste buds are still there. You still know how to turn them on, right?"

"I suppose I do, but why bother?" He popped the last bite in his mouth.

Surprise zinged through her. "Do you mean to tell me you don't taste *anything* anymore?"

"Not really." He pointed to her sandwich. "Are you going to eat that or not?"

"No." She shoved her window open and quickly pitched the sandwich out. "And I'm not going to watch you eat it, either."

"Hey."

"Hey. Forget it. And surely there's *something* you still like to eat."

He shrugged. "I like eating Juliana's pie."

A stinging tendril of jealousy whipped through her. "Who's Juliana?"

"Griff's wife." He smiled. "She loves making apple pie."

A *married* woman. A woman married to a man almost as handsome as Rand. She could live with that. "Okay, you like Juliana's pie. What else?" There had to be something else. She couldn't imagine someone completely forgoing, on a full-time basis, something as enjoyable as eating.

He thought.

And thought.

"Come *on*. You have to be able to come up with more than one thing you still bother to turn your taste buds on for."

He shook his head. "Sorry."

Sadness and irritation coiled through her. It made her sad to think the man had given up on his dream and seemed to go out of his way to deny himself even the slightest pleasure. Particularly since he was denying himself for a job he seemed to hate. But running right alongside that sadness was irritation. Who was he to tell her she was responsible for her own happiness when he didn't even know what he liked to *eat* anymore?

Man. Someone needed to give him a good swift kick.

She smiled wickedly. And maybe, just maybe that someone should be her.

Chapter Fifteen

Rand sat on a log he'd pulled up next to the fire, warming his hands and admiring Winnie's wildflowers as they swayed gently in the evening breeze. It was late Saturday evening. Twenty-one hundred to be exact. The new watch had just gone on duty.

He rubbed his hands together trying to stave off the chill. He'd pulled on a light jacket earlier, and he would pull on a heavier one soon. By morning he would be wearing several layers and he'd still be cold. His body just wasn't adjusting to these temperatures.

He peered into the woods, watching. Nieto's men had been spotted in Canada this morning, but the woods were quiet here. Everything was quiet. With neither packages nor mail to pick up or deliver, Winnie hadn't left her cabin today. Which was maybe a good thing.

He was glad he'd convinced her their kiss and his job were two separate entities. Glad he'd erased the sense of betrayal she'd felt over it. But by doing so he'd also lifted the barrier between them her anger had provided. And that could be a dangerous thing.

Despite his determination to stay detached, professional, he couldn't look at her without wanting her. Being shut up in that tiny plane with her yesterday, seeing her begin to discover her real self, listening to her laugh, feeling the sexual energy flow between them—despite the fact they'd both studiously ignored it—had been an exquisite torture. It had almost been a relief to sit here all day with her locked up safe and sound in her little cabin. Safe from Nieto's men. Safe from him.

He did wonder what she was doing in there, though. She'd been pretty industrious all day. Flitting around in the kitchen. And a couple of hours ago Talon had shown up and delivered a paper bag to her. The kind used at grocery stores. Rand had asked what was in it, but Talon had just shrugged and headed back to his post.

Rand shook his head and tossed another log on the fire. Talon was a damned good soldier. A man he liked having at his back in the field. No one fought with more skill or do-or-die determination than Talon. But if one was looking for conversation or information, Talon was useless.

The American Indian looked upon the world with a jaded sense of humor and, on the whole, kept his own counsel. Neither gossip nor casual observations crossed his lips. If he was privy to some information he thought someone really needed to have, he told them. Beyond that, he was silent.

Since he hadn't shared what was in Winnie's bag, Rand could only assume the contents were harmless. But he would have liked to know what she'd gone to the trouble of calling for. He didn't like that she was working behind his back. And she obviously was.

After all, he could have taken her to the grocery store. And the only reason he could think for her not wanting him to do so was that she didn't want him to know what was in that bag. He poked at the fire with a stick and then glanced at the house. What *was* she up to?

He didn't think she'd be stupid enough to try to shake her guards, but he wasn't certain. She was being a pretty good sport about the guard dog routine, but he knew she still wasn't completely happy about it.

He glanced back at the cabin. It was easy to see inside. The light was starting to fade outside, and she'd turned the inside light on about half an hour ago. So it didn't take long to locate her. She was still in the kitchen. Currently taking something out of the oven, if he wasn't mistaken. Sitting here close to the ground, he couldn't see what it was.

He stood up, but not quickly enough. She was

already settling a big hand towel over it. Whatever it was, it was odd shaped and lumpy. Some type of baked goods he would guess under normal circumstances. But these were anything but normal circumstances.

She brushed her hands off on the back of her jeans and then strode toward the front door. The pine portal swung open and she leaned out, a teasing smile on her lips. "How's it going out here? All quiet on the Western front?"

He ignored the warm rush her smile brought and nodded. "Very quiet."

She rubbed her hands together, mischief sparkling in her eyes. "Pretty chilly out here."

His senses went on full alert. She was definitely up to something. "So I noticed."

She looked up at the stars beginning to appear in the sky. "Supposed to be colder tonight than last night."

He sighed. "Did you just come out here to torment me?"

She chuckled. "No. Actually, I came out to offer you a warm place to sleep tonight."

Heat shot through him as the picture he'd spent the entire day trying to keep at bay leaped into his head—Winnie and him together, naked, in bed. He was quite sure that wasn't what she had in mind. And he damned well couldn't act on it even if it was.

The more practical side of his brain slowly kicked into gear. While he'd set up camp outside because he hadn't wanted to invade her space, he would much prefer to guard her from inside. And he wasn't going to knock a little warmth, either. "A warm place to sleep?"

She nodded. "I thought you might like to sleep in here tonight. Where it's warm. Where you could sleep on a soft sofa instead of the cold ground."

"Is this an invitation?"

"Maybe."

He raised a brow. "Maybe? I take it there's a catch."

She nodded, her smile getting a little wider. "You have to pass a test."

Wariness slid through him. "What kind of test?"

"Come on in and I'll show you." She disappeared into the house.

He grabbed his rifle, strode through the wildflowers in her front lawn and followed her into her tiny abode. The smell of cinnamon and fresh baked goods assailed him the minute he crossed the threshold. He took another breath of the aromatic air. "You've been baking."

"Yep. That's your test." She waved a hand to where the dish towel covered its lumpy treasure. "Apple pie."

He raised a questioning brow. "Apple pie is my test?"

She nodded. "Here's the deal. Tonight we're going to wake your taste buds up a bit. I think you've gone on in this phase of—I don't even know what to call it, really—self-denial, maybe? But whatever it is, enough is enough. I'm sorry you have to eat icky things sometimes. But that's no excuse to forsake the joys of food altogether. So tonight we're going to reacquaint you with the pleasure of eating.''

There were a million pleasures he'd thought about sampling as he'd stood outside her house and stared in, thinking of her. Eating apple pie wasn't at the top of his list. Hell, it wasn't even on the list. But that was the last path he should be going down, so he kept quiet while she continued.

''You said you liked apple pie. And since I just happen to make the best apple pie this side of…well, it used to be the Mississippi, but I guess now it would be the Canadian border.'' She waved away her moment of distraction. ''Anyway, since I make such a bang-up apple pie, I thought that would be the best way to wake up your poor neglected taste buds.''

''Well, I can certainly eat apple pie for a place on your sofa, no problem.''

She chuckled devilishly. ''Oh, no, it's not going to be quite that easy. I saw you gobble that awful sandwich down with a smile on your face. If all you had to do was eat the pie you probably wouldn't bother to taste anything.''

He cocked a brow. ''I take it there's another catch.''

Her smile got a little more wicked. ''Absolutely.'' She whipped the dish towel off the baked goods on the table. ''As you can see there's more than one pie here. There are actually two pies. One I baked. And a frozen one I had Griff send over from the store.''

"So that's what was in the grocery bag Talon showed up with a few hours ago.''

She nodded. "Yep. Pie and ice cream.''

He lifted a brow. "Anything else in there?''

She shot him a quizzical glance. "In the bag?''

"Yes.''

"No.''

"You're sure?''

She tsked. "I'm sure. Why? What do you think was in there? A bomb?''

"Since you're offering me apple pie, I was thinking something more subtle. Sleeping pills. Or strychnine maybe.''

She rolled her eyes. "For pity's sake, Rand, one of your men delivered it. Do you really think he would have brought me something I could create havoc with?''

"As a general rule, no. But with Talon one can never be sure. His sense of humor is a little twisted.''

"Well, it's apparently not that twisted. There were neither sleeping pills nor strychnine in the bag. And besides, what on earth would I use either of those things for? I'm not mad at you anymore.''

"And I'm glad to hear that. But I'm not so sure you've completely accepted the guard dog routine.''

She shrugged. "I'm not thrilled about it. But I'm much less thrilled about the thought of facing

Nieto's men by myself. So I won't be feeding sleeping pills to you or anyone else in Griff's little army.''

"Glad to hear it."

"I'm sure you are. Now, back to the pies. This is the test. I'm going to have you taste each pie, and you have to guess which pie is mine and which is the store-bought one. Guess wrong and you'll be sleeping on the ground again. But guess right—'' She waved a hand toward her sofa "—comfort and warmth.''

She'd thought this test out carefully. He was actually going to have to taste each item in order to win his place inside. No chewing and swallowing without tasting just so he could smile and tell her how wonderful it was regardless of its culinary value.

Equally worrying was the fact that if he didn't actually choose hers, the best apple pie this side of the Canadian border, he was not only going to find himself back outside, she was going to be mad at him. Again. He sighed. "You're a devious woman, Winnie Mae Taylor.''

She chuckled softly. "I know. Now, go sit down on the sofa. I'll get you blindfolded and we can begin.''

"Blindfolded? Oh, no. I can't protect you if—''

She shot him a disparaging look. "Oh, please. Relax for a few minutes, will you? Cash and Talon are right down the road, right?''

"No, Marshall and Rawlins are down the road.

Cash and Talon packed it in at twenty-one hundred. But—''

''Well, I'm sure *whoever* is down the road has things under control. Besides I'm not going to tie you up—just put a blindfold over your eyes. If Nieto's men manage to show up during the test, you can jerk the thing off and start shooting.''

He hesitated, but only for a moment. As long as he could dispose of the blindfold in a moment's notice he supposed there was no real harm in it. ''Okay. Let's play your game.'' He strode to the sofa, leaned the rifle where it would be close at hand, slipped his jacket off and sat down.

She snatched up a red bandanna from the coffee table and kneeled beside him on the sofa, her knee pressing into his thigh. ''Close your eyes.''

He closed his eyes and she leaned closer, tying the bandanna around his head. Darkness enveloped him, intensifying his other senses. Intensifying the feel of her knee pressing into his thigh. Her breasts brushing his shoulder. Her heat soaking into his side.

Need, hard and hot, made the fit of his pants tight and his fingers itch to reach out and touch the soft flesh pressing against his shoulder. He gritted his teeth and resisted the urge. Definitely not a professional thought.

''Relax. This isn't going to be hard.''

A humorless laugh echoed through his head. It was already hard. And he wasn't talking about her little test.

She gave the knot on the bandanna a last tug and

then pushed away. He heard her shuffling around as she brought the pies over and set them on the coffee table. The smell of cinnamon and warm crust intensified. And then she was sitting beside him again, her body pressed against his.

He ruthlessly ignored the jolt of need that shot through him and tried to concentrate on the task at hand. Figuring out which pie was which.

"Here's the first bite."

He smelled the pie as a forkful of it was thrust under his nose. He opened his mouth and she popped it in. He chewed slowly, concentrating on the taste.

A bit of a sweat broke out on his forehead as he realized maybe he *didn't* know how to turn his taste buds on anymore. The tastes he was experiencing weren't very distinguishable.

If he didn't do better than this he was going to disappoint her for sure. He concentrated harder. Okay, it was sweet.

Salty.

Mushy.

Gooey.

Edible, but nothing spectacular. God, he hoped this one wasn't Winnie's. He swallowed.

"Good?" Winnie asked the minute his Adam's apple bobbed back into place.

Uh-oh. Did her enthusiasm mean it was her pie? He was in serious trouble here. "It was good," he assured.

"Okay. Now taste this."

He opened his mouth and another bite was forked in. He chewed slowly again, praying there would be a huge difference between the last bite and this one. That this one would obviously be Winnie's amazing apple pie. Or so bad he'd know for sure her pie was the other one.

It was sweet. Salty. Mushy. Gooey. Exactly like the last one from all he could tell. He swallowed. Hard.

"Well?" she demanded.

Oh, man, why had he ever agreed to this? He thought fast. "I'm pretty sure I know the difference. But I think I need one more bite of each to be sure."

"You're kidding, right?" Indignation sounded in her voice.

He winced. "Just one more bite of each and I'll know for sure."

She snatched the bandanna from his eyes. "Rand, these two pies are as different as night from day. If you need one more bite to tell which one is store bought you're not trying."

He tried desperately not to notice how good it felt to have her body pressed against his, her skin rubbing against him, her heat... Enough. "I am trying, it's just that... Look, don't take this personally, but, I'm not sure I ever really liked apple pie."

"But you said you *did* like it," she said in a disappointed whine.

"Actually, I didn't. What I said was, I liked to *eat* Juliana's pie. But not because it tastes good."

Her brows snapped together in bafflement. "Why *else* would you eat it, for pity's sake?"

"Because Juliana has so damned much fun making it. Baking is a new experience for her, apparently. And apple pie was the first thing she baked for Griff, so she likes making it."

"But it's good, right?"

He shrugged. "How would I know? I don't taste it. I eat it the same way I eat everything else. Two chews, a good swallow and a happy smile."

She shook her head. "You're hopeless, you know that? You're probably missing a really great treat."

He shook his head. "I seriously doubt it. No one else at the compound will touch it."

That baffled look crossed her face again. "Then why do *you* eat it?"

He shrugged. "Because Juliana puts such effort into it. *Someone* should appreciate it."

She chuckled softly, shaking her head. "You're a sweet man, Rand Michaels. A bit of a sap. But very sweet. Don't let anyone tell you differently." She patted his thigh, a simple, friendly gesture.

But his body took it as a whole lot more than friendly. His pulse kicked up a notch, and the fit of his pants, already uncomfortable, became downright painful. He needed to get out of here before he was permanently injured. Or before he did something he'd truly regret.

He lifted her hand away and cleared his throat. "Listen, this was a nice idea you had, but I think it would be best if we called it quits and I go back outside.'' Where the cold temperatures would cool his ardor and she'd be out of his reach. Because right now he wanted nothing more than to pull her across his lap and pick up where their last kiss had left off.

She grabbed his arm and shook her head. ''Oh, no, you don't. You can't call it quits now. You've barely started.''

''Winnie—''

''Look. I'm not going to let you quit until you give this a legitimate try. You want to turn your taste buds off in the field, fine. But here, now, I want you to taste what's in front of you. Good food is pleasurable. Joyful. Sensual even. And there's no reason for you to cut it out of your entire life just because it's unpalatable on some occasions.''

Fresh need pounded through him. If he didn't get out of here now, they were both in trouble. And being tactful obviously wasn't going to get him out. He locked his gaze on hers. ''You want to know what's pleasurable?'' He tipped his head, all it took to bury his nose in her hair, and drew in a deep breath. ''The way you smell, warm and purely female, is pleasurable. Joyful?'' He pointed to where their bodies touched. ''Your skin against mine. Sensual? The feel of your breast snuggling against my arm. You want to talk about taste? I could give a good damn about tasting either one of those pies. But I want to taste you so badly I ache. And if I don't go now, *right now,* I'm going to do it.'' He waited for her to let go, leap from the sofa and run to a safe distance.

But she didn't. Her fingers tightened on his arm. Her breathing picked up, shortening to erratic, whispering pants that skated over his cheek. Her gaze skimmed away and then snapped back. "What if I want you to?"

"Oh, Winnie."

Her pink little tongue darted out and wet her lips. "I do want you to. I don't know where either of us is going to be when this is all over. But I want you to kiss me again. I want to feel that electricity. That heat. That earth shaking need."

He shouldn't do it. He should get up and walk out of this room. Now, while the getting was good. But he couldn't do it. He didn't even want to do it. What little restraint he had evaporated like water in a steam engine.

He closed his lips on hers, his tongue delving into her mouth, exploring, claiming, tasting. He pulled his lips away just far enough to whisper to her. "Now this is a taste worth savoring. Sweet. Sexy. Intoxicating." He tasted again, reveling in the soft silkiness of her mouth.

She leaned into him, a soft moan vibrating on her lips as she gave him free access, her arms wrapping around his neck, trying to pull herself closer.

He needed her closer, too. A lot closer. He lifted her, pulling her to him.

She followed his lead, straddling him, settling onto his lap, her knees on either side of his thighs, her warm feminine core snuggling against the hard proof of his desire.

His turn to moan…and pull her closer, his hips thrusting gently against her. *Yes.* He settled his hands at her hips, setting a slow provocative rhythm that would drive them both to distraction…and the gates of heaven.

His tongue dived deeper.

She leaned closer, her breasts pressing into his chest, her fingers plowing through his hair.

His hands shook. He cursed the denim beneath his fingers as he guided her through another teasing thrust. She was so soft, so hot, so…giving.

She wasn't like the women he'd dreamed of all those years, she *was* the woman. And he wanted…*needed* to taste that. Just once. Then if he died tomorrow, he could die a happy man.

A very happy man.

The need to strip them both naked and sink into her warm, silky flesh was stronger than his need to breathe. But, heaven help him, what about her? One night with a woman like Winnie was more than he'd ever thought he'd have. It would be a gift. A blessing. A precious memory he could carry around with him for the rest of his lonely life. But Winnie had a future ahead of her. What could he give her?

Nothing. He didn't have a damned thing to offer. Except regret. And he'd already given her enough of that. His hands tightened at her hips and he stole one more taste. One more deep, long, heavenly taste for the lonely future waiting impatiently in the wings. And then he dragged his lips from hers and pushed her hips back from his. His breathing hard and ragged, he shook his head. "We can't do this."

Her fingers sank into his shoulders, her brows crinkling in distress. "What's wrong?"

He shook his head. "Everything. You don't want a one-night stand, Winnie. And that's all I have to offer."

"I'm not asking for a lifetime commitment, Rand. Just—"

"I know you're not. But it's what you want."

"How do you know what I want?" Frustration sounded in her voice.

He laughed, a short, humorless burst of sound. "Winnie, you spent four years trying to hold a marriage together that didn't have a chance for happily-ever-after. A one-night stand would never be enough for you. And I'm not going to risk hurting you because we're both too hot and bothered for our own good." He set her from him and pushed off the couch.

She stared at him from the sofa, frustration and hurt in her eyes.

His own body ached with unfulfilled need. *Dammit,* if either of them got out of this in one piece, it would be a damned miracle.

He grabbed his coat and rifle and strode toward the door. "Once I'm out of here, lock this door behind me and don't open it for anyone." Least of all him.

Chapter Sixteen

Winnie hefted the big packing box onto her bed. She'd left half her stuff in boxes when she'd moved here, anticipating another move when she found that other job. The better-paying one. But she wasn't looking for that job anymore. So today she was unpacking.

It wasn't the most interesting thing a person could be doing on a bright, sunny Sunday afternoon. But she wasn't up to facing Rand this morning, and she needed *something* to keep her mind off last night's kiss. She was frustrated and confused and edgy.

Part of her was glad Rand had pulled away before they'd gone any further. He was right, she didn't go to bed with men easily. If she went to bed with him she'd give him part of her heart. And she wasn't at all sure she was ready for that. And yet…

And yet part of her wondered if she hadn't missed something really…magical last night. She'd never felt the intensity of need, of emotion that had all but exploded between them.

But was one night of magic enough for her? Because it was clear Rand wasn't willing to give her more than that. Didn't think he *could* give her any more than that. At least not much more than that. If he'd taken her to bed, she thought he probably would have stayed there until the mission was over. But beyond that, she knew he intended to leave.

Of course, she didn't have to stand by and watch him leave. She could ask him to stay. But that would mean risking an even bigger part of her heart. Particularly since there was no guarantee he would stay even if she asked. In fact, all indications pointed to the opposite. And she was definitely not ready for that kind of heartbreak. She was just starting to piece her heart back together as it was.

She sighed as she ripped off the duct tape keeping the top of the box closed. Enough. She wasn't going to think about it anymore. After thinking about it all night long, lying in bed wide awake, her body aching with unfulfilled desire, her brain needed a rest.

She was going to concentrate on the tiny part of her life she had decided on. Turning her little cabin into a home. She opened the top of the box. It was filled with odds and ends. She lifted the short stack of school yearbooks out of one corner and set them on the bed. She would carry them out to the book-shelves in the living room in a bit. Next came a couple of heavy brass bookends. Steerman biplanes doing mirror image loop-de-loops. She smiled, setting them on the bed. It would be nice having those out where she could see them again.

From another corner she picked up something wrapped securely in a towel. Obviously something she hadn't wanted to get damaged. She unwound the towel from the square object. Her jewelry box. She smiled again. This was definitely lifting her spirits. It was a little like opening presents on Christmas morning.

She set the box on her dresser. There weren't many places to wear jewelry out here, but she had a few pieces she really liked. Casual pieces she could wear almost anytime. Just to add a little sparkle to her day. She opened the lid and peeked inside. There was the simple gold chain with the single pearl her mother had bought her for her sixteenth birthday. Next to it was the class ring she'd wanted so badly…and worn for a week. And the watch Tucker had given her not long before he'd left.

Her heart hitched, a sharp reminder of just how painful risking her heart could be. She picked up the watch, her fingers hesitant and a little bit shaky. The gold was smooth and cool to her fingertips.

It had been the last gift Tucker had given her.

She rubbed the watch between her fingers, old memories sifting through her mind. The engraving on the back of the watch's face caught her attention.

She flipped the watch over and stared at the name engraved in fancy, flowing letters. A name that was not hers.

Wait a minute. An ugly suspicion snaked through her. Tucker'd had an excuse for the name at the time he'd given it to her. An excuse she'd readily believed. But now, thinking back on that time from a very different perspective, she wasn't so sure she believed it anymore. She wasn't sure at all. Particularly when she thought about the way Tucker had rifled through the jewelry box that last day. Was this what he'd been looking for?

Pain and anger sliding through her, she strode out of her bedroom, through the living room and pulled open the front door.

Rand turned to her, his rifle cradled in his arms.

She waved him over. ''Come here.''

He strode through the wildflowers in her small yard, rifle in hand. ''What's up.''

She held the watch up so he could see. ''About eight months ago, when Tucker came home for one of his short visits, he gave me this.''

He looked down at the watch, then back to her. It was clear from his expression he wasn't sure what she wanted from him. ''Very pretty.''

She smiled wryly. ''Isn't it, though? But that's not why I'm showing it to you.''

He raised a brow. ''Why *are* you showing it to me?''

She did her best to ignore the pain squeezing her

chest. "Because I'm not sure it was meant for me. In fact, I don't think it was."

"Why not?"

She tried to remember exactly what had happened the day Tucker had given her the watch. She shook her head. "Because the events surrounding his giving me the gift are odd...."

His gaze sharpened. "How so?"

She hesitated, unsure where to start.

"Winnie, just start talking. We'll work through what's important and what's not later."

"Okay. It was the second day Tucker was home. As usual I'd made a big dinner for his arrival the night before. There were a ton of leftovers I thought we'd have for lunch. But when lunchtime rolled around he made this big deal about wanting a peanut butter sandwich." She shook her head at her stupidity. "A peanut butter sandwich! I'm such an *idiot*. Who eats peanut butter once they're over twelve?"

"Actually, I think there are a lot of people over twelve who still eat peanut butter."

"Well, Tucker never ate it before. The jerk." She should be mad, but she just felt drained. "He obviously just wanted me out of the house. And like a good little wife, I zipped off to get him his peanut butter." She shook her head again. "But I'd barely made it down the block when I realized I didn't have any cash. So I zipped back to the house to get some."

"Is this where the watch comes in?"

She nodded, her surety that Tucker had duped her

that day solidifying. "When I went back into the house, he was wrapping a small jewelry box in pretty pink paper. He looked up, obviously surprised and disconcerted at my arrival. When I asked him what he was doing, he stumbled around for a bit, but then said he'd brought a gift for me and he'd been hoping to get it wrapped before he gave it to me. But since I was already there...and knew about it, he might as well just give it to me."

"So he gave it to you?"

"Yeah."

"I take it the watch was inside the box?"

She nodded again, a cold knot forming in her stomach. "I fell in love with it the minute I saw it. Not just because it was pretty. But because it was the first time he'd brought me anything from one of his trips. I was thrilled. And then I noticed the name engraved on the back wasn't Winnie Mae."

"And you asked him about it?"

She nodded, her throat constricting as she realized how easily Tucker had manipulated her.

"What did he say to that?"

"Said he hoped I wouldn't mind the inscription on the back. He explained it wasn't a new watch. He'd seen it at a flea market on his last mission. Said the minute he'd seen it he'd thought of me. And he didn't think I'd mind the engraving."

"And you believed him?"

That cold knot got a little bigger. "At the time, yes."

"And now?"

"I think I intercepted a gift meant for his new sweetie. I remember being surprised at how new it looked at the time. There wasn't a scratch on it." She stared at the watch, trying to ignore the empty feeling in her stomach. She'd already realized her marriage had been over long before Tucker put an actual end to it. It was silly to let these bits of proof upset her so much. And yet, every piece of evidence stung anew.

She rubbed the watch between her finger and thumb one last time and then handed it to Rand. "Maybe it's the clue that will help you track him down."

He flipped the watch over, his gaze snapping to thin, brown bands as he read the inscription.

"What do you think?"

"Carmen Marguerite. Fairly common names alone, but together a bit unusual. And the fact that they're both Latin American strikes a cord. Not only did Tucker disappear from South America, but according to the CIA he worked exclusively in that area for the last year or so. This might indeed be the clue we need to find him. Let's give Griff a call, see what it turns up."

He handed the watch back to her, unclipped the cell phone from his belt, punched a button and held the small, slim phone to his ear. He waited only a second before he started talking. "This is Michaels. Winnie just showed me a watch Tucker gave her about seven or eight months ago. It's got the name Carmen Marguerite engraved on the back. It's a long story, but Carmen Marguerite might be the woman Taylor ran off with.''

He paced away a few steps, listening. Then he nodded his head. "Okay, we'll be waiting to hear back." He snapped the phone closed and turned back to her. "Griff's going to call the CIA, see if they come up with anything. And since the CIA doesn't always share information, he'll have one of our guys at Freedom Rings checking, too. He'll let you know as soon as he hears anything."

She nodded, staring out at the snow-capped mountains in the distance. She'd given Rand her clue. She should go back inside. Continue to unpack. But she couldn't find the energy to get her feet to move.

His eyes narrowed on her. "You okay?"

She forced her lips into a smile. "Yeah, fine." But she wasn't fine. She felt cold and drained and…alone.

He watched her a few seconds, looking concerned. "I'm sorry about the watch."

"Not your fault I married a rat and couldn't figure it out." She felt awkward just standing there. She could tell he was waiting for her to go back inside. But she couldn't face the silence waiting for her inside. Not right now.

Rand sighed. A sigh that clearly said he was about to say something he knew he shouldn't. "Do you want me to come in for a while, keep you company?"

She should say no. It was obvious he was trying

to keep his distance. And until she knew what she wanted to do about him, keeping some distance between them was probably a good idea. They seemed to be a bit volatile when they were together. But right now, right at this moment, with yet more proof of Tucker's betrayal burning in her hand, she didn't care. She needed company. And Rand Michaels was the best company she could think of on any given day.

She stepped out of the doorway, holding the door open. "Yeah. I'd like that."

It was late. Past ten and they were sitting at the kitchen table playing gin. A game Rand had made clear he thought was a sissy's game. But Winnie hadn't been up to learning the rules behind poker and he'd known the rules to gin, so she'd twisted his arm, and he'd agreed to play.

He'd been great company. He'd chased the cold and loneliness away. Kept her from thinking about her dismal past. Kept her from thinking about what was going on outside this cabin. The hunt for Tucker.

A thread of pity slipped through her. They hadn't heard anything from Griff, but she could feel things changing, coming to a head. For the first time since this had all begun she'd moved beyond her bewilderment and anger at Tucker to think of the sad end he had created for himself. Jail if he was lucky. Death if he wasn't.

God, what had he been thinking?

She shook off the melancholy thoughts and re-focused her attention on the cards in her hand. If she drew the right card next, she might actually win this set.

The cell phone sitting conspicuously in the middle of the table rang.

Both of their gazes snapped to the small plastic box.

It rang again.

Rand snatched up the phone and flipped it open. "Yeah?" He listened quietly for a few minutes, his expression tight. "Okay." He snapped the phone closed, his gaze meeting hers. "You hit the jackpot. They think they've found him."

"With Carmen?"

He nodded, his expression knowing, subdued.

She swallowed hard and made herself ask. "Who is she? When did he meet her?" It didn't really matter, of course. That part of her life was over. Finding out all the nasty little details would only be rubbing salt into the wound.

But she wanted to know.

"She was an agent for the Colombian government. She and Tucker first met almost two years ago, when they worked a case together."

Two years ago. The cold and loneliness started to creep back in. "I see. Where are they?"

"Amsterdam. At least Carmen is there. And they're pretty sure Tucker is with her."

"Pretty sure? What does that mean?"

"It means the agents on the case haven't seen him

with their own eyes, but the locals in the area say Carmen is staying with an American. One whose description is a dead ringer for Tucker. They're assuming it's him.''

''Amsterdam,'' she mused. ''Seems an odd place for a South American and Tucker to run to. He was always partial to tropical climates.''

''Not so odd. Apparently Carmen Marguerite has a half sister living there, so they had a place to go to ground. And Amsterdam has an anonymous banking system much like Switzerland's. You want to hide lots of money, Amsterdam's a good place to be.''

Ah. The chill spread a little further. They'd obviously been planning this a long time. ''So how did they find them so fast?''

He shrugged. ''The CIA has agents in every country in the world, just waiting for little jobs like this. And the Colombian government knew about the half sister. She's Carmen's only living relative, so it was a good place to start. A little surveillance turned Carmen up right away. And a couple of discreet but pointed questions indicated Tucker was probably at hand, as well.''

She nodded, the swiftness with which the case was coming to a close knocking her off balance. ''How soon before they actually capture them? And what about the money? How will they recover that? I seriously doubt Tucker's just going to hand over the bank account number.''

''Let Uncle Sam worry about the money. Trust

me, he has his ways. As for Tucker and Carmen, the CIA thinks they'll have them by tomorrow morning—at the latest.''

Despite knowing Tucker had chosen this path for himself, sadness washed over her. ''I wonder what pushed him over the edge?''

''What made him steal the money?''

She nodded.

''It's not unusual for agents to cross the line. In the field the lines of right and wrong become blurred. Sometimes they seem to disappear altogether. It's during those moments when the lure of money can drag an agent over.''

''It's sad.''

He reached across the table and took her hand, letting her know she wasn't alone. ''Yes, it is. But it was his choice, Winnie. One he freely made. With full knowledge of what would happen to him if he got caught.''

''I know.'' She did her best to push the melancholy thoughts away.

Rand gave her hand another squeeze. ''The up side is, within hours of Tucker's and Carmen's capture, the CIA will have word to Nieto that they were responsible for the theft of the money. And that Uncle Sam has them safely in custody. Within hours of that Nieto will have his men off your tail. Providing we haven't scooped them up by then. You'll be safe again.''

Safe. It sounded good. Except…

It meant Rand would be leaving. Soon. If things

went smoothly, he could be gone by tomorrow night. Maybe sooner.

A trill of panic fluttered in her breast. She wasn't ready for him to leave. Not yet. She pushed up from the table and paced anxiously across the kitchen's old linoleum, the raw emotions of the day crashing together. Anger, betrayal, sadness, loneliness. They all joined together, becoming a giant, roaring wave of pain and uncertainty that threatened to drown her.

She gasped for air.

Suddenly Rand was behind her, his strong, comforting hands taking hold of her shoulders, stopping her frantic pace, steadying her. "Easy. You're trying to suck in too much oxygen. Slow down."

She turned to him, grabbing hold of the soft flannel of his shirt. He was like an anchor in the storm. Steady, strong. Warm. She leaned into him. Drinking in that heat, that strength.

He hesitated only a moment before closing his arms around her. "It's okay, I've got you."

Yes, he did. She could feel the wave receding. But she knew the second he let go it would come back. She didn't want that. Couldn't face it. Not tonight. She didn't know what the future would bring. Didn't know what decisions she was going to make tomorrow. But she knew what she wanted right now. Knew what she needed.

She didn't let herself think. Didn't let herself hesitate. She looked up at him, her fingers tightening in his shirt. "I want you to stay tonight."

He gently brushed a curl from her cheek. "Don't

worry, I'm not going anywhere until Nieto's men are off your tail. I'll be right outside your door."

"That's not what I mean. I want you to stay here, in my house." She hesitated, her nerve threatening to flee. She'd never asked a man to sleep with her before. But she held on to her courage and clarified her meaning. "In my bed."

Raw desire flashed across his face. But then panic flashed in his eyes. He snatched his hands from her shoulders as if they had suddenly caught fire and stepped back, shaking his head. "We already went over this. You're not a one-night-stand kind of woman. And—"

"And I don't care about any of that. Not tonight. I need you. I want to feel the way you make me feel. Special. Prized. I need that. I'm not asking for a lifetime commitment. I'm only asking for one night. One night where neither of us has to feel lonely or sad. We deserve that. Both of us. Please."

Chapter Seventeen

*P*lease.

The word echoed in his head. It was the sweetest invitation he'd ever heard. But he shouldn't accept it. He *wasn't* what she needed. He sure as hell wasn't what she deserved. He drew a breath to protest again.

But before he'd spoken a word, she placed her finger over his lips. "Shhh. Don't be noble tonight. Let us have a night of pleasure and joy and let tomorrow take care of itself." She replaced her fingers with her lips. Lips that sipped at his with shy encouragement and bewitching entreaty as she leaned closer.

Her breasts pressed into his chest. The feminine

curve of her hips snuggled against his. Heat and
need short-circuited his brain. But it was the dream,
the dream of having a woman as beautiful and sweet
as Winnie Mae Taylor in his life that short circuited
his conscience. He groaned and pulled her closer,
answering her kiss with a more aggressive one of
his own.

She kissed him back, her arms wrapping around
his neck, her body stroking his. And then she pulled
her head back just far enough to uncouple their lips.
"Is that a yes?"

If he was going to stop, this was the moment. But
his fingers refused to let go of her, and his body
ached at the thought of pushing her away. He
wanted this night. This single night to chase the
darkness away from all the dark, lonely nights
ahead.

The moment ticked by. "Yes," he whispered, just
before he closed his lips over hers. He kissed her
deep, drowning in the taste of her, the feel of her.

She answered his kiss eagerly, her tongue dancing
with his, her body straining toward him, moving
against him. With a final hungry kiss and a low
groan she pulled away.

"Please don't tell me you changed your mind."

She put her finger to her own lips this time.
"Shhh. Come on." She grabbed his hand and pulled
him toward the short hall that led to her bedroom,
a shy smile hovering on her lips.

His heart squeezed. Leading men to her bed was
obviously new to her. He felt honored that she

should choose to do so with him. Honored and aware that he wanted to make this night as special for her as he knew it would be for him. He followed her eagerly, his body throbbing, his heart aching. Aching with something frighteningly like love.

He closed the door on the emotion immediately. Love was about happily-ever-after. Endless tomorrows. Shared eternity. He had only tonight to offer.

Winnie pulled him into her room and shut the door behind them, creating a dark, secluded lovers' bower. Moonlight shone through her window. The thought of seeing her bathed only in the silver light sent more heat pouring through him. But he strode across the room and pulled the window shade down. His fellow soldiers were in those woods, watching the house, keeping it safe. He had no intention of sharing this night with them. He found his way back to her in the dark and pulled her into his arms.

Her arms twined around his neck as she leaned into him, her lips opening to his, her tongue darting out to invite his inside. Yes. Winnie Mae Taylor in his arms. He'd dreamed about this from the moment he'd seen her. And now she was here. Warm. Soft. And so damned sweet.

He angled his head and deepened the kiss, tasting her, devouring her. But it wasn't enough. It would never be enough. He slid his hands down to her hips, pulling her against the neediest part of him.

Heat and a desire so sharp it threatened to take him to his knees crashed over him. The clothes had to go. He needed her naked, under him, around him.

His lips still locked on hers, he let go of her hips and started working his buttons open.

Winnie grasped his intention immediately. She pulled her arms from his neck and went to work on the buttons dancing down her flannel shirt, their knuckles bumping together as they worked at getting naked.

Their shirts hit the ground with a soft sigh, and then their knuckles bumped lower as they went to work on their jeans. Thirty seconds later, shoes and socks had been toed off in a flurry of bumping knees and tangled limbs, and their pants had been kicked off behind them.

Too impatient to wait to feel her skin against his, to allow time to shuck their underwear, he pulled her close. Soft, silky skin met his. He deepened the kiss, a thousand tantalizing images of Winnie naked flashing in his head. Smooth, alabaster skin. Her sexy little backside. Glorious, full breasts. Need pounded through him. If he was going to have only this one night he wanted to see the real thing.

He dragged his mouth from hers. "We need some light. I want to see you." His voice was as hard and rough as his need.

She whimpered softly as he pulled away, her fingers holding on to him until the last second. "There's a lamp on the nightstand by the bed. Hurry."

He made his way around the bed in the dark. When his knees bumped the small piece of furniture, he felt for the lamp with a shaking hand. Locating the shade, he reached beneath and turned the switch. Light infused the room, quite bright at the nightstand but dissipating rapidly as it spread through the chamber, leaving the corners in shadow while a soft glow washed over Winnie.

Winnie.

She was even more beautiful than he'd imagined. Ten times more beautiful, with her soft curves and her creamy skin and her shy smile. She was wearing baby-pink cotton underwear. High-cut bikini panties and a simple bra. Some men might prefer French lace, but there was an innocence about the pink cotton, a normalcy that was far more arousing for him than French lace would ever be. Heat poured through him.

His body pulsing with need, he strode back to her. Starting at the tip of her shoulder, he ran a finger over the delicate line of her collarbone. "Beautiful. So damned beautiful." Everything about her was beautiful. And perfect. Except…

He gently traced the skin over the white bandage on her arm. "I'm sorry about this. I'm so sorry."

She shrugged, a graceful dip of her shoulders. "It wasn't your fault."

He looked away from her, guilt clawing at his hide. "Of course it was."

She caught his chin with her fingers and pulled his gaze up to hers, her green gaze locking on to his. "Stop it. Tonight isn't about anything that happened before this moment. It's about now. About you and me and pleasure and joy. Remember?"

Yes. A single, precious memory for the future. "I remember." He took her hand and led her the few steps to the bed. "I want to see all of you."

She hesitated only a moment before she unhooked her bra, slid the straps from her arms and dropped the small scrap of material to the floor.

He swallowed hard. "Did I say beautiful?" His hands shaking, he cupped her fullness, testing, exploring. "Beautiful doesn't even come close. Extraordinary, maybe. Glorious. No…perfect," he whispered in a reverent sigh and closed his mouth over a perfect pink nipple.

Heaven.

She leaned into him, a soft sigh whispering from her lips.

He drew harder.

Her fingers dug into his arms. "Rand." It was a desperate plea.

One that echoed in his own blood. He wanted to taste every inch of her, memorize every curve. But it would have to wait. Right now he wanted all of her. Needed all of her. He pulled his mouth from her and divested himself of his last piece of clothing. He stood before her naked, aroused, a final warning of where they were going. He held his breath. Would she stay? Or rethink her decision and flee?

She didn't even hesitate. Her eyes darkening with desire, her pink tongue darting out to moisten her lips, she slipped her fingers beneath the elastic of her pink panties and shimmied out of them. Locking her gaze on to his, she stepped up to him, skin to skin, wrapped her arms around his neck and closed her lips over his.

Heat exploded within him. With a soft groan he pulled her closer and sank onto the bed, bringing her with him. The mattress dipped beneath them as she settled over him, her soft little body sliding against his. Soft and willing and so, so hot.

She moved against him, her full breasts branding his chest. One leg slid up his flank as she molded her body to his, opening her intimate heat to his aching need.

He deepened his kiss and thrust forward, not into her, not yet, but into the soft, slick folds guarding her feminine entrance, his hardness stroking over the tight little bud that controlled her pleasure.

She moaned deep in her throat and thrust back, her arms tightening around his neck. He grasped her hips, guiding her against his hardness, helping her find what she needed. What they both needed.

With her weeping heat wrapped around him, his own need threatened to spiral out of control. But he wasn't going to let that happen. Not with this woman. He rolled them over, taking the top position for himself. Propping himself on his elbows he stared down at her. At the luminous green of her eyes, the shiny curls of her hair, the lush fullness of her lips.

So beautiful.

She smiled softly. Her knees snuggled against his hips. Her womanhood gently nudged the head of his arousal. Reaching up, she gently ran a finger down his jaw. "Take away the cold, Rand. Please."

She didn't have to ask twice. He slid forward, slow and easy, sinking into her to the hilt.

She arched under him, taking him deeper, claiming him as surely as he claimed her. A sigh of pure ecstasy whispered from her lips. Her fingers tightened at his shoulders.

He pulled back and stroked again, harder this time. Deeper.

She shuddered beneath him, her body already tensing for its release, her tightness closing around him like a hot, slippery glove.

He clenched his fists. "Neither of us is going to last more than ten seconds."

She smiled up at him. "But it's going to be a damned good ten seconds."

Yes, it was. He got down to business, gathering her close and setting a rhythm that would appease instead of tease.

She writhed beneath him, her arms pulling him closer, deeper, her hips driving against his, matching him thrust for thrust. "More." The breathless command whispered from her lips. "I need more of you."

He gave her what she wanted. What they both wanted. He drove into her again and again, hard and fast, leading her, taking her, driving her to the top.

He heard the tiny scream that started in the base of her throat and worked its way up as she dug her nails into his back and arched high against him.

He closed his mouth over hers, capturing the sound. He wasn't sharing that sweet cry with anyone.

And then her body snapped taut as an archer's bow, and with a final cry, she shuddered in his arms, her body convulsing around him, her arms squeezing him tight.

And not a moment too soon. He surged into her, taking as much of her as he could get as he crashed over the top right behind her.

Winnie's breath, as hard and fast as his, warmed the juncture between his neck and shoulder, her arms wrapped tightly around him.

He reveled in her. Savored the way they fit together. Relished the light and warmth she gave him.

A tendril of fear flicked through him. The light and warmth wouldn't last. When he left, the numbing emptiness of his life would be back. With a vengeance.

He swallowed against the panic surging up his throat and tightened his arms around her, hanging on to the light, the warmth, the goodness that radiated from her. She was in his arms now. And now was all that counted.

He flexed inside her. He wanted more. Needed more. But just because he was ready didn't mean she was. He gently thrust forward, testing the waters.

She shuddered beneath him and lifted her hips toward his, a dreamy need darkening her gaze. "Do that again."

"Absolutely." He thrust again, memorizing every

detail. The soft curve of her lips. The half-lidded, smoky look in her eyes. The greedy arch of her body beneath his. He wanted this night to last forever. He gently pushed the hair from her face and traced the small curve of her ear. ''Conserve your energy, lady. It's going to be a long, long night.''

She shot him a sexy grin. ''I'm going to hold you to that promise, soldier.'' She gave her hips a wicked twist and pulled his mouth down to hers.

He made love to her all night long—with the light on so he wouldn't miss a touch or a sigh or the tiniest expression. So he would remember...

Everything.

Chapter Eighteen

Winnie snuggled against Rand, her head pillowed on his shoulder, her breasts pressed against the solidness of his rib cage, her leg thrown over his. He was warm and comfortable and, she suspected, awake—despite the fact his eyes were closed, and he lay unmoving. She wondered if he feigned sleep to prevent the night from ending. She certainly didn't want it to end. It had been the most incredible night of her life. She'd never felt so wanted or cherished.

She shivered just thinking of the way he'd touched her. His hands moving over her as though worshiping her and memorizing her at the same time. And the way he'd watched her... She shivered again. His heated gaze had caught her every sigh, her every move.

She didn't want this time to end. But she could feel the end coming. The first rays of dawn were peeking around the window shade. The new day was upon them.

As though sensing her thoughts, Rand's arm tightened around her, drawing her closer. He opened his eyes, his gaze moving to the window. "The sun's coming up. I'm going to have to go soon." His voice was rough with spent passion and regret. Regret that the night was coming to a close.

The same panic she'd felt last night at the thought of him leaving filled her again. Only bigger this time. Much, much bigger. She held him tighter. "I don't want you to go."

He dropped a kiss on her forehead. "I don't want to go. But we can't stay here forever. The world is waiting, and I should be outside when the watch changes."

She could feel him pulling away from her. Feel him slipping back into his professional world. The world where he felt he belonged. The panic got stronger. "If you go back out there, you aren't coming back in, are you?"

Shadows rolled across his face. "No."

"Then I don't want you to go out there. Let the guys in the woods take care of Nieto's men."

The corners of his mouth tightened. "It's my job, Winnie. I have to go back out."

"No, you don't." She sounded like a petulant child, but she didn't care.

He looked down at her, shadows filling his eyes. "Winnie, stealing one more day isn't going to make us feel any better when it's time for me to go."

The truth of his words hit her like a jet punching through the sound barrier. He was right. Twelve more hours would never be enough to calm the emotions roiling inside her. The panic crawled up her throat. She'd shied away from the questions bombarding her about Rand for the past few days. But she'd just run out of time. If she was going to ask him to stay, now was the moment. Because if he left this room he'd be gone for good.

The thought of asking terrified her. Between her father and Tucker she'd had enough rejection to last her a lifetime. And asking Rand to stay was definitely setting herself up for another rejection. He'd made it clear he didn't think he belonged in a woman's life. Even for a little while. Convincing him to stay wouldn't be easy.

Her heart squeezed. The only other option was to sit quietly by while he walked out of her life. Is that what she wanted? Did she want to let him leave before they even had a chance to find out if the magic they'd shared last night could become something truly wonderful?

Sounded an awful lot like victim mentality to her. And she was through with that. She drew a deep, fortifying breath and took the plunge, reaching for the first time in her life for something *she* wanted.

"What if I want more than one more day? What if I want you to stay after the mission is over?"

Tension rippled through him, the arm cradling her becoming stiff. Frustration and unhappiness clouded his gaze, but he did his best to temper his emotions as he looked down at her. "Winnie, last night was wonderful. Extraordinary. But as much as either of us might want it to go on, it doesn't have a future."

Her stomach tightened, but she wasn't going to give up. She'd stood idly by while her marriage had fallen apart. She was going to fight for what she wanted this time. "I'm not asking for forever. Just…just a little more time to see if there's a future out there for us."

His lips tightened, the shadows in his eyes darkening. "You've chosen a beautiful place to start your new life, Winnie. Don't ruin it by trying to drag me into it. I don't belong here."

Her heart pounded against her ribs. "Why not? Because you think you don't belong in a domestic setting? That's ridiculous. I've seen you with the people here, Rand. They like you. The people on my route like you. Henry likes you. The *sheriff* likes you, and it's his job to tell the good guys from the bad guys. If you gave yourself half a chance you'd fit in here beautifully."

He grimaced, rolling away from her and out of the bed. "The people here don't know me." He strode toward his discarded clothes with that fluid, panther grace of his.

She swallowed hard and tried desperately not to

let all that hard muscle and naked skin and glorious, raw maleness turn her brain to mush. "They do know you. They might not know the soldier half of you. But they know the other half. The half that likes Alaska and likes to fish and even seems to enjoy sitting over ice cream and cookies for a friendly chat."

He pulled on his briefs and snatched up his jeans, irritation starting to show on his face. "That half doesn't count."

"Yes, it does." She pulled the sheet tight around her, leaped out of bed and headed for her own clothes. If he thought he was going to dress and just walk out of this room, he was wrong.

She snatched up her panties and struggled to put them on without dropping the sheet, her mind turning frantically. If she didn't figure out a way around his ridiculous nobility she was sunk. They were sunk. Because she thought he wanted this as much as she did. He was just afraid to...

Afraid?

She stilled, one foot in her jeans, one out. Where had that notion come from? He had never said he was afraid of anything. He'd said he didn't want to bring the ugliness of his past into someone else's life. She couldn't shake the feeling that some brief blip of intuition had led her to an important piece of insight. But what could he possibly be afraid of?

The man was a mercenary. An ex-CIA operative. What on earth could possibly be scarier than that?

The dread clawing at her hide gave her a hint.

Part of her mind laughed at the thought, loudly claiming any man who had faced down drug lords, armies and who knew what other nasty foes couldn't possibly be afraid of something as trivial as rejection. The other half told her to check out the cold sweat on her palms, the pounding of her own heart if she thought it was such a minor thing.

Lord, her delusional, desperate mind might be making it all up. But it was the best plane on the field. She was going to fly it. She glanced at him. Yikes. He already had his pants on and was buttoning his shirt. Once he stomped into his boots he'd be ready to bolt. And she had no doubt in her mind he was going to.

She abandoned the sheet in favor of a quick hop into her jeans. Then she snatched up her shirt and dashed for the door. Once she was firmly established in front of it, she pulled on the crumpled flannel. She didn't bother to button it, she had more important things on her mind. She just overlapped the material and crossed her arms over her chest. "You know, the day you told me why you didn't think you belonged in the civilian world, why you thought you couldn't have a wife and family, I wondered if your decision was selfless and wise—or cowardly and unutterably stupid."

"And what did you decide?" His tone made it clear he didn't care which answer she'd chosen as he jerked his socks on.

"I think maybe both. I got a good sample of how caring you are after the crash and—"

He snorted at the comment. "I was just doing my job."

"Maybe. To a certain extent. But your job certainly didn't include patrolling for bears. And you did that."

"Only because it made you feel better," he said, stomping on his boots.

"My point exactly. You care about other people's feelings. Which leads me to believe part of you is indeed being noble when you say you don't want to bring what you perceive as the ugliness of your life into the life of the average Joe. But I also think part of the reason you're staying at a job you clearly hate is cowardice."

"Good for you." He snatched up his rifle and strode over in front of her. "Now step aside."

She shook her head. "I'm not done yet."

"If you're going to expound next on why you think I'm a coward, I assure you, I don't care."

She took a deep breath, holding on to her resolve…and her temper. "Good. Then you won't mind listening to it. I think you've had to make decisions and do things in your work that you're ashamed of. Decision and actions that—"

"Shame is the least of my worries. I've made decisions and done things that will give me nightmares for the rest of my life."

She could see the pain in his eyes. A pain she wished she could chase away. A pain she wished he would give her the *chance* to chase away. "I stand corrected. And while I believe you wouldn't want those decisions, those actions to give anyone else nightmares, I also think part of the reason you won't chance a normal existence is you're afraid of rejection.''

He cocked a challenging brow. ''You think I care if some neighbor decides he doesn't want to talk to me?''

''No. But I do think you would care—very much—if the woman you wanted to build that dream of domestic bliss with decided she didn't want to talk to you. That she couldn't handle your past and didn't want to share your life anymore. The other day I said that if you told a woman about your past after you fell in love, and as long as she loved you, as long as her love was strong enough, you could still have your dream. But I didn't stop to think how you'd feel if her love *wasn't* strong enough. I didn't stop to think how you might feel seeing the remorse you feel about your past reflected back to you in the eyes of the woman you love. I think fear of that rejection is the real reason you went back to the trenches.''

His lips pressed into a hard line. ''You don't know what you're talking about.''

She noted the hard set of his jaw, the anger sparking in his eyes. And if she looked behind that anger, she thought she saw panic. ''I think I do. In fact, I think I hit the nail on the head. But if you stay, if we decide we might have a future, you're not going to have to worry about me discovering your past. I know you're a mercenary. I know you're ex-CIA.

Your past isn't going to blindside me. Or frighten me."

"Glad to hear it. Now if you're done psychoanalyzing me, will you please step out of the way?"

Stubborn, stubborn, *stubborn*. She wanted to shake him until his teeth rattled. Last night had meant as much to him as it had to her. She was positive it had. She'd seen it in his eyes, felt it in his touch. And still he was determined to close the door on it and walk away without ever looking back.

Well, she wasn't ready to do the same. "Not yet."

He took an intimidating step forward and leaned over her, his eyes narrowing to thin bitter bands. "You might think you know what's in my past. You might *think* you know what being a mercenary or a CIA operative is all about. But, sweetheart, you don't have a clue. I could tell you stories that would make your hair stand on end and your stomach heave."

She flinched, but she didn't back down. She met his gaze head-on. "I'm sure you could. And if it would make you feel better to tell them to me, I wish you would. I'd like to see some of the shadows skulking in your eyes leave, or at least lighten up a bit. But the stories won't make me run. Or think less of you."

Anger and frustration flashed in his eyes. "Do you think I don't want to stay? That if I thought for one second I could give you what you needed I wouldn't stay?"

She tossed her hands in the air. "Just what do you think I need?"

"Someone like yourself. Someone as innocent— as good—as you are. And I am not that man."

She leaned toward him, locking her gaze on his. "Rand Michaels, you *are* that good man. You're not only a good man, you're the best man I've ever known. You're kind and gentle—"

He snorted in disdain. "Kind, gentle men do not have an ocean of blood on their hands."

"Some of them do. The heroic ones do. Men who have fought for our freedom on the battlefield and behind it. Men who have sacrificed their own peace so that others could have it. Those men have an ocean of blood on their hands. But it doesn't make them bad or uncaring or—"

"Christ, don't make me out as a hero."

"Fine. But don't make yourself out as a monster, either. Don't you see?" She splayed her hands in supplication. "It's the ugly things you've lived through that make you look at the mountains and see not only their grandeur but their peacefulness. That make you appreciate the simplicity of a little cabin in the woods. That make you touch me with such gentleness."

He spun away from her, his hands gripping his rifle so tightly she was surprised it didn't crush beneath his fingers. "Why are you doing this? Why are you making this so hard?"

She stared at his retreating back in frustration. *Because I love you, you pigheaded*— Oh, God.

Her heart stopped. The *world* stopped as realization crashed over her.

She loved him.

She loved him. She wasn't fighting this hard because she wanted him to stay for a week or a month or until they figured out if they had a future. She was fighting this hard because she wanted him to stay...forever.

Fear pounded through her. Dear God. She'd known she would risk a piece of her heart if she went to bed with him. But she hadn't lost merely a piece of it. She'd lost it all. Though, she suspected, a huge portion had been lost long before last night. After all, a man who loved his fishing rod, a man who patrolled for bears without a whimper when he no doubt thought he could use his time better spitting into the wind was a hard man to resist.

She stared at him, taking in the tension vibrating through him, the hard press of his lips, the conflicted, almost tortured look in his eyes. He was so determined to leave. So determined to spare her, him, both of them, an ugly scene in the future.

Her heart pounded a frantic tattoo. She could feel him slipping through her fingers. If she didn't do something fast she was going to lose him.

Stay, please stay. I love you. The words hovered on her lips. But she didn't say them. She wouldn't say them.

She'd spent her whole life begging for someone's love. Her father's. Tucker's. She wasn't ever going to do it again. If Rand stayed she wanted him to do it because he wanted to. Not because she pushed him into it. Or begged him for it. But because he loved her.

As much as she loved him.

Heart and body and soul.

But there was one thing she could point out. She locked her gaze on his. "You know, Rand, a wise man once told me people are responsible for their own happiness. That they should figure out what they want in life and go out and get it. If you go back to Freedom Rings you deserve every bit of misery you get. Every bit of misery that type of life has to offer. On the other hand, if you want something better—much, much better—now's the time to reach out and grab it." Drawing a deep, steadying breath, she stepped away from the door.

He started toward it.

A shot rang out, the sound cracking in the woods close to the house.

Oh, God, Nieto's men had found their way to Alaska.

Chapter Nineteen

"Get down." Rand grabbed Winnie and pulled her down behind the bed. Once he had her safely stashed he made his way to the window and peeked beneath the shade. Nothing. The yard and woods surrounding the house were empty. He snatched the radio from his belt and jammed the talk button down. "This is Michaels. What's going on out there?"

"I don't know yet." Cash's voice crackled over the radio. "The shot came from Marshall's quadrant, but he hasn't checked in."

Not unusual, Rand knew. If Marshall was playing hide-and-seek with a shooter in the woods, he wouldn't want the squawk of the radio or his voice to give his position away.

"I'm on my way out there now," Cash's voice crackled over the radio again. "We might just have a hunter who's fallen over a log with his safety off, but let's not count on it. Until you hear from me, assume the worst. You got a nice little closet you can secure our lady in?"

Rand stared at the closet across the room. It didn't have an outside wall in it. "You bet."

"Good. I'll be in touch."

Rand zipped back to Winnie in a half crouch and took hold of her elbow. "You heard the man. Let's go."

"Oh, no." She tried to pull out of his grasp. "There is no way you're going to stuff me in that closet. I'll feel like a sitting duck in there."

He held on tight, dragging her across the room, doing his best to keep her low as she struggled against him. "You won't be a sitting duck. You'll be in the securest spot in the house. And I'll be right outside the door, making sure it stays that way."

Her eyes popped wide. "You think I'm going to hide in there while you stand out here and get shot at? No way." She struggled harder.

"For crying out loud, Winnie, Nieto's men aren't here to play games. Get in the damned closet." Giving up all pretense of diplomacy, he used brute strength to drag her to the closet and stuff her in.

She slammed her feet against the door just as he

tried to close it. "You want that door shut you get in here with me."

"Don't be ridiculous. I have—"

"You're not going to stand out there and get shot for me, Rand. *Get in.*" Her mouth was set in a mutinous line. Her eyes sparkled with pure determination. Obviously, if he didn't get in that closet with her they were going to fight about it for the next ten minutes.

He didn't want to fight about it one more second. He wanted another wall between her and the bullets being thrown around outside. And his attention needed to be on what was going on outside the cabin, not inside it. "Fine. Move over." He could protect her as well from inside the closet as out. He moved into the small space, closed the door behind him and hunkered down, his rifle braced across his knees. If anyone came into this room and opened the closet door without identifying themselves, he'd be dead before he finished turning the knob.

Adrenaline pounded through him, bringing his senses to full alert, readying him for battle. His eyes adjusted to the pitch-blackness of the closet.

Winnie scooted over by him, her shoulder bumping his. "What's going on out there?" she whispered, worry and fear vibrating in her voice.

He wrapped one arm around her shoulders, absorbing her heat, taking what comfort he could from the fact that she was currently unhurt. "Don't worry. Whatever's happening, our guys will handle it. No one's going to hurt you."

"I don't want *anyone* to get hurt."

He squeezed her harder. "I know you don't." But he couldn't promise her that. No one could. When bullets starting flying, all bets were off.

Another shot rang out.

Winnie jumped with the sharp retort.

Another shot. And another.

So much for the lone hunter theory. The battle was on.

He drew her closer. "Easy. I've got you." For all the good that might do her. Even with the best armies, under the best of circumstances, things went wrong. People died. The innocent right along with the guilty.

He prayed to God it wouldn't happen today. His arm automatically flexed, bringing her closer. He drank in the feel of her. Her warm skin. Her goodness. Her sweet, loving nature.

A single shot suddenly crashed through the bedroom window and hit the closet wall with a solid thunk.

"Dammit. Get on the floor." He pushed her down, making her lie flat.

Another shot crashed through the window and hit the outside wall of the closet. Another punched through the wall, a thin shaft of daylight marking its entrance into their haven.

"Quick, scoot as close to the back wall as you can." He quickly maneuvered in the tight space, stretching his body over hers, urgency clawing at his gut.

She stiffened the moment his body settled on hers. "Oh, no, you are *not* going to be my body armor. Get off me." She bucked up, trying to dislodge him.

He pressed down harder with his body, squelching her attempt to crawl out from under him. "I'm not getting off, Winnie, so lie still, dammit. And be quiet. I need to hear what's going on outside so I'll know if I have to get up and start shooting."

Another bullet smashed through the closet wall, bringing the threat of violence and impending death with it.

She stopped struggling and flattened out as close to the floor as she could get, her muscles rigid with fear. "Oh, God."

The darkness closed around them, the air becoming heavy, hard to breath. He waited for the moment when he would have to pick up his rifle and kill someone. Waited for the burning pain created when a bullet tore through flesh.

God, he was tired of it.

Tired of the violence. Tired of the killing. Tired of it all. And the thought of losing one more innocent person, *the thought of losing Winnie,* threatened to suffocate him where he lay.

Something inside him moved, shifted, snapped. He couldn't stomach the violence any longer. And he couldn't bear the thought of leaving Winnie. Not for the madness that raged outside the cabin.

Not for anything.

He buried his face in her hair. Her wild curls tickled his nose, and he breathed in her soft, sweet smell. He wanted this. He wanted *her*.

But did he have any business with her? Even if she could handle his past, why should she?

A cold laugh echoed through his head. Winnie was right. He was afraid. The last thing he wanted to see was her looking at him with rejection in her eyes. And what the hell did he have to offer her that would make it worth her while to put up with the baggage he would bring with him?

Winnie's words rang in his ears, louder than the gunshots outside. *Don't you see? It's the ugly things you've lived through that make you look at the mountains and see not only their grandeur but their peacefulness. That make you appreciate the simplicity of a little cabin in the woods. That make you touch me with such gentleness.*

He thought of the loneliness he'd seen in her eyes when she'd spoken of her father. The sadness and anger when she'd spoken of Tucker. Maybe he did have something to offer her.

Maybe.

The gunfire escalated outside, rising to a frantic pace. It sounded like a full-out war out there.

And then…silence.

The sound of their breathing filled the closet.

His radio crackled to life. "We're clear. You can let her out now," Cash said.

It was over. And she was safe. Thank God. He grabbed his radio and jabbed the talk button down.

"Roger that." He stood, bringing her with him. "Let's get out of here."

Winnie followed him out of the closet, gulping in giant breaths of oxygen and praying her knees wouldn't give out. She had never been so scared. Or so angry.

Tightening her grip on Rand's hand, she gave it a mighty tug, pulling him around to face her. "What in God's name were you thinking, throwing your body over mine? You think I want to live with your death on my conscience?"

He pulled her to him, wrapping his arm around her in a comforting embrace. "Winnie, we're both fine. No one died in there. No one even got hurt in there."

No, no one had died. But they'd come danged close. Too close. The fragility of their lives stole her breath. And brought reality crashing in on her with startling clarity. The stupid commercials were right, life was short. Too short not to say what was in your heart. What the other person did with that knowledge was their business, their decision. But she wasn't keeping secrets anymore.

She leaned back and locked her gaze on his. "I love you. If you don't love me enough to give us a chance, well, I think that's your loss. But I'm not fooling around. I love you, right down to my shaking little bones. And I think you should stay in Alaska. With me. I think we have a chance at something really special. Something really magical."

She held her hand up, forestalling any objections he might have. "But if you don't think so, if you really don't want to stay, fine. But please, *please* think very hard before you go back to that life." She pointed to her window, indicating the shattered glass and the mayhem that had gone on just outside her cabin.

To her surprise he didn't tense up. A frown didn't crease his brow. In fact, a hint of a smile crossed his face as he looked steadily into her eyes. "As a matter of fact, I've thought very hard about it. And I'm not going back to that soulless existence. Never again."

Her breath caught. A tiny ray of hope flickered to life. "You're not?"

He shook his head, his smile getting a little wider. "No."

Hope and fear sizzled through her. "Planning to go anywhere specific, then?"

He shrugged, mischief sparkling in his eyes. "Didn't think I'd go anywhere. Thought I'd stay right here. See what happens."

She wanted to jump with joy, but she held off. They'd just been through a pretty tense experience. She wanted to be sure he'd thought this through. She wanted to be sure he *wanted* to stay. And she wanted to be sure he was committed. She didn't want him staying if he wasn't going to give them an honest chance. "You're not afraid? Afraid you'll taint my life? Or that I'll discover something horrible you've done and walk out on you?"

His expression turned serious, and he swallowed hard. "Scared spitless. There's no use kidding you. It won't be easy, Winnie. There are parts of my past, ugly parts, that won't ever go away. They'll be with us forever. But if you're willing to give me a chance, I'll make it worth your while. A day won't go by that you won't know I love you."

Her world stopped. Joy threatened to burst inside her. "Could you repeat that?"

He tucked an errant curl behind her ear, his smile returning. "Oh, yeah, did I forget to mention that? I love you, Winnie Mae Taylor, right down to your shaking bones and your sweet, sweet heart." He kissed her then, his lips playing softly over hers. A soft, gentle kiss of banked passion and yearning hope.

She leaned into him, reaching for more. More passion. More hope. He deepened the kiss, closing both arms around her.

His rifle poked her in the back.

With a giddy chuckle she pulled back and tipped her head toward the offending weapon. "You *are* going to get rid of that, aren't you?"

"I thought I'd trade it in."

She raised a brow. "Yeah? For what?"

He shrugged those big, sexy shoulders. "A fishing rod." He hesitated, his look becoming almost...bashful. "And maybe a few kids."

Kids? The hope that had been growing by the moment burst in a giant ray of joy. If he was thinking kids, he was committed. Big-time. She gave him a beaming smile. "Going to teach them how to fish?"

He smiled back, his expression getting more confident by the moment, the shadows in his eyes lightening up with each second that passed. "They're gonna need something to do when they're not in the air doing loop-de-loops with their mom."

Her heart squeezed. Old skills and old traditions being passed down from one generation to the next. "Yes, they will." She hugged him tight, drinking in his heat. His strength.

His love.

"We're lucky people, Rand Michaels. Lucky, lucky people. And we're going to have such memories...."

Epilogue

"Happy birthday!" The whole room reverberated with the jubilant cry.

Griffon Tyner stood off to the side in Winnie's living room, sipping at a beer and watching Jennifer Mallard close her eyes, make a wish and blow out the candles on her birthday cake. She was a cute kid, he thought. All freckles and young, thirteen-year-old mischievous smiles. In a few short years he imagined she'd be leaving broken hearts in her path right and left.

Griff took another sip of the cold brew, watching Rand give the girl a hug and hand her a present to unwrap. There was a table loaded with them, one from every person filling Winnie's small cabin.

Winnie had thought a big birthday party was the perfect way to celebrate Jenny's new teenage status. And to introduce Rand to the small Alaskan community. And if the abundant turnout was any indication, she was right.

Of course, Griff had helped with the attendance, using his helicopter as an air taxi for those who'd wanted to come. It had made for a hectic morning, but he'd wanted to meet the people, too. Get a feel for the place Rand planned to call home.

He'd known Rand for years. He liked him, respected him, understood his demons. He wanted to be sure he was leaving him in good hands. The party was the perfect opportunity for that. And his men, who'd been invited to the festivities, as well, could use the day to relax before they returned to the Freedom Rings compound. Before the next job put them back in danger's path.

The last two days had been hectic as they'd wrapped up the case on Winnie's ex. There had been mountains of paperwork, local and federal, to do on Nieto's men, both of whom had gone down in the gun battle. Tucker and Carmen had been picked up in Amsterdam by the CIA and were currently being held in federal custody to await trial. Griff was pretty sure they'd both be using canes long before they saw the light of day through anything other than prison wire.

Most important, for Winnie's sake, the money had been recovered, and Nieto had been informed that his fifty million dollars was safely tucked in Uncle Sam's pocket.

Unfortunately, the powerful drug lord hadn't been apprehended yet. But Griff felt certain that day would come. He hoped sooner rather than later. But Winnie was safe, and Rand could rest easy knowing the fifty mil that had disappeared on his watch had been recovered.

Winnie cut the chocolate cake, put a piece on a plate, grabbed up her pop can and headed his way. Stepping up to him, she offered him the birthday sweet. "I wanted to thank you for watching out for me and doing everything you and your men did to keep me safe."

He tipped his head. "Anytime."

"So what do you think of our little party?"

"Very nice." He looked back to Rand. He was watching Jenny open her presents while he talked to an older woman with a long gray ponytail. "Rand seems to be enjoying himself."

Winnie turned her gaze to Rand, her expression softening, a knowing smile pulling at the corners of her lips. "Yeah, I think he is. He was worried about fitting in here. But he's going to fit in. He's going to fit in really well."

"He's a good man. Anyone would be privileged to call him friend. But don't underestimate the impact his past is going to have on some people. A lot of people think the CIA is the evil empire. And most people have a pretty low opinion of mercenaries."

She dipped a delicate shoulder. "I know. But he

doesn't need a city full of friends, just a few good ones.''

"You're right, a few good friends will do. The person he's really going to need acceptance from is you. How do *you* feel about his past?''

She narrowed her eyes on him and chuckled softly. "Why, Mr. Tyner, are you watching out for one of your men?''

"Always.''

She shook her head, smiling wryly. "I'll tell you the same thing I told him. His past isn't going to chase me away.''

"How much do you know of his past?''

"Not much. But he has shared a couple stories with me over the past two days. I think he's testing the waters. Seeing if I'll freak out and bolt.''

"And?''

"And do I look like I'm getting ready to bolt?''

No, she didn't. She looked poised and confident. But... "He wouldn't have started with the tougher ones.''

"No, I'm sure he didn't. But the tougher ones won't scare me away, either.'' Her gaze met his, steady and unwavering. "I love him, Mr. Tyner. Do you have any idea what that means?''

A few months ago he would have had to say no, he didn't know anything about love. But then his wife, Juliana, had come into his life with her steely determination, loving heart...and their precious daughter. She'd shown him how strong a person's love can be. Shown him how love can transform a man from an empty shell to a living, loving human being. "I know what loving someone means." He raised his beer bottle. "I wish you both well."

"Am I missing a toast?" Rand joined them, dropping an arm around Winnie's waist and pulling her close.

"Yep. But now you can join us." Griff lifted his bottle again. "To love, happiness and fish the size of boats."

Winnie and Rand laughed, tapped their drinks and drank.

"Speaking of fish," Rand said. "Mary said Grant McKinley, one of the local outfitters, needs a fishing guide. Thought I'd wander over there tomorrow, see what he's looking for."

Winnie smiled up at him, mischief sparkling in her green eyes. "Fishing guide? I thought you'd learn to fly. Be my copilot."

Rand smiled right back. "Are you kidding? I thought I'd go to work for McKinley, learn the area while I teach you to fish, and then you and I would open up a mom-and-pop outfitter shop."

Pure devilment shone from Winnie's eyes. "Keep hoping, bud. In the meantime, how do you feel about wing walking? We could become a new air show sensation."

Griff laughed. It looked as if Rand was going to have his hands full. It also looked as if his soldier was in good hands. Very good hands, if the naked love shining in Winnie's eyes as she stared up at the ex-mercenary was any indication. Good. It was about time Michaels moved on.

"Major." Cash stepped up to the group, his expression much more grave than the party demanded.

Griff's senses went on alert. "What is it?"

"I just heard from the compound, sir. Matt missed his ride. They thought you should know."

Damn. Not good news.

"Who's Matt?" Winnie asked, concern knitting her brow.

"One of my men," Griff answered. "He's out of country trying to get a senator's daughter and four orphans out of a hot zone. They were supposed to meet one of our helos this morning. Apparently, they didn't make it."

"Should I collect the men?" Cash asked.

Griff nodded and then held his hand out to Winnie. "It's been a pleasure, ma'am. Either of you ever need anything, give me a call." He turned to Rand, took his hand and laid his other hand on his shoulder. "Take care of her. She looks like she's going to be the best catch of your life. And keep in touch. Juliana and I will expect periodic reports." He shook Rand's hand and followed Cash and the rest of his men from the party.

It was time to go back to work.

He took one last look behind him. Rand and Winnie were wrapped in each other's arms, kissing. Griff smiled. The mercenary business was a brutal one, one where even success was oftentimes hidden in death and despair. It was a business where good endings were hard to come by.

But this...

This was a good ending.

A very good ending.

* * * * *

Coming soon from

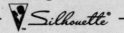

SPECIAL EDITION™

MONTANA MAVERICKS

THE KINGSLEYS
Nothing is as it seems beneath
the big skies of Montana.

DOUBLE DESTINY
including two full-length stories: FIRST LOVE by Crystal Green
and SECOND CHANCE by Judy Duarte
Silhouette Books
Available July 2003

Moon Over Montana by JACKIE MERRITT
Available July 2003 (SE #1550)

Marry Me…Again by CHERYL ST.JOHN
Available August 2003 (SE #1558)

Big Sky Baby by JUDY DUARTE
Available September 2003 (SE #1563)

The Rancher's Daughter by JODI O'DONNELL
Available October 2003 (SE #1568)

Her Montana Millionaire by CRYSTAL GREEN
Available November 2003 (SE #1574)

Sweet Talk by JACKIE MERRITT
Available December 2003 (SE #1580)

Available at your favorite retail outlet.
Only from Silhouette Books!

Where love comes alive™

Visit Silhouette at www.eHarlequin.com   SSEMMAV

eHARLEQUIN.com

Sit back, relax and enhance your romance with our great magazine reading!

- **Sex and Romance!** Like your romance *hot*? Then you'll *love* the sensual reading in this area.

- **Quizzes!** Curious about your lovestyle? His commitment to you? Get the answers here!

- **Romantic Guides and Features!** Unravel the mysteries of love with informative articles and advice!

- **Fun Games!** Play to your heart's content....

Plus...romantic recipes, top ten lists, Lovescopes...and more!

Enjoy our online magazine today— visit www.eHarlequin.com!

INTMAG

If you enjoyed what you just read,
then we've got an offer you can't resist!

Take 2 bestselling love stories FREE!

Plus get a FREE surprise gift!

Clip this page and mail it to Silhouette Reader Service™

IN U.S.A.
3010 Walden Ave.
P.O. Box 1867
Buffalo, N.Y. 14240-1867

IN CANADA
P.O. Box 609
Fort Erie, Ontario
L2A 5X3

YES! Please send me 2 free Silhouette Special Edition® novels and my free surprise gift. After receiving them, if I don't wish to receive anymore, I can return the shipping statement marked cancel. If I don't cancel, I will receive 6 brand-new novels every month, before they're available in stores! In the U.S.A., bill me at the bargain price of $3.99 plus 25¢ shipping and handling per book and applicable sales tax, if any*. In Canada, bill me at the bargain price of $4.74 plus 25¢ shipping and handling per book and applicable taxes**. That's the complete price and a savings of at least 10% off the cover prices—what a great deal! I understand that accepting the 2 free books and gift places me under no obligation ever to buy any books. I can always return a shipment and cancel at any time. Even if I never buy another book from Silhouette, the 2 free books and gift are mine to keep forever.

235 SDN DNUR
335 SDN DNUS

Name	(PLEASE PRINT)	
Address	Apt.#	
City	State/Prov.	Zip/Postal Code

* Terms and prices subject to change without notice. Sales tax applicable in N.Y.
** Canadian residents will be charged applicable provincial taxes and GST.
 All orders subject to approval. Offer limited to one per household and not valid to current Silhouette Special Edition® subscribers.
 ® are registered trademarks of Harlequin Books S.A., used under license.

SPED02   ©1998 Harlequin Enterprises Limited

New York Times Bestselling Author

LISA JACKSON

A TWIST OF FATE

When Kane Webster buys First Puget Bank, he knows he is buying trouble.
Someone is embezzling funds, and the evidence points to Erin O'Toole. Kane
is determined to see her incriminated—until he meets her. He didn't expect
to feel such an intense attraction to Erin—or to fall in love with her.

After her divorce, Erin has no desire to get involved with anyone—especially
not her new boss. But she can't resist Kane Webster. Before she can help it,
she's swept into a passionate affair with a man she barely knows...a man
she already loves. But when she discovers Kane's suspicions, she must
decide—can she stay with a man who suspects her of criminal intent?

"A natural talent!" —*Literary Times*

Available the first week of June 2003 wherever paperbacks are sold!

Visit us at www.mirabooks.com   MLJ705

SPECIAL EDITION

#1549 PATRICK'S DESTINY—Sherryl Woods
The Devaneys

Warmhearted kindergarten teacher Alice Newberry couldn't help but be drawn to rugged fisherman Patrick Devaney. The easygoing high school football star had become a brooding loner…but Alice was determined to get behind Patrick's gruff exterior to the loving man she knew was inside.

#1550 MOON OVER MONTANA—Jackie Merritt
Montana Mavericks: The Kingsleys

Some would have called it love at first sight—divorcée Linda Fioretti knew better. Just because carpenter and single dad Tag Kingsley was warm, open and charming, didn't mean she had to trust him with her heart…but the more time she spent with him, the more she wanted to.

#1551 AND BABIES MAKE FOUR—Marie Ferrarella
Manhattan Multiples

Jason Mallory was shocked to see high school sweetheart Mindy Richards—single and pregnant…with twins—sitting at his administrative assistant's desk! But despite the years apart, Mindy and Jason still wanted each other. Would they take their second chance at true love…and the family of their dreams?

#1552 BALANCING ACT—Lilian Darcy
Readers' Ring

When widowed dad Brady Buchanan and single mom Libby McGraw realized their adopted daughters were twins, they knew they had to do what was best for the girls—keep them together. Fate had brought Brady and Libby to each other…. Could this unconventional family find a way to stay that way?

#1553 HIS BROTHER'S BABY—Laurie Campbell

When lawyer Connor Tarkington escaped to his family's vacation home, he found beautiful Lucy Velardi, and her baby daughter, abandoned by his irresponsible brother. Living under the same roof, Connor and Lucy soon realized that maybe they'd found just what they needed—in each other.

#1554 SHE'S EXPECTING—Barbara McMahon

Mandy Parkerson wanted a job far away from the man who had spurned her and their unborn child. Jackson Witt worried that his new pregnant secretary would remind him too much of the family he'd lost. A love that surprised them both had the potential to heal their past hurts…and lead them to a lifetime of passion!

SSECNM0603